The man screamed in pain and terror the instant the snowtrack slammed upright on its treads at the bottom of the fifty-foot-deep crevasse, driving his spine upwards, breaking it in several places. The heavily laden sled with its cargo of canisters came tumbling down on top of him, the hammering clatter filling his ears. Then he could hear a hissing noise coming from one of the canisters; it was leaking.

With a burst of inhuman strength, the man managed to move; to actually edge a few inches away from the leaking canister.

Death, the single, horrifying thought crystallized in his mind before his eyes glazed over. And then his throat began to swell; the nerves throughout his entire body began to thrum like a guitar string. He went totally berserk, his body thrashing and jerking uncontrollably, his broken spine ripping and severing key blood vessels, muscles, and nerves; his broken ribs punctured his lungs in half a dozen places; and at last, his tongue protruding from his chattering mouth, he bit completely through it, the blood pumping out, almost instantly freezing in the unbelievably cold antarctic temperature, while above, the storm raged. . . .

NICK CARTER IS IT!

FROM THE NICK CARTER
KILLMASTER SERIES

*Dedicated to the men of the
Secret Services of the
United States of America*

NICK CARTER

OPERATION: McMURDO SOUND

CHARTER
NEW YORK

A Division of Charter Communications Inc.
A GROSSET & DUNLAP COMPANY
51 Madison Avenue
New York, New York 10010

First Ace Charter Printing June 1982
Published simultaneously in Canada
Manufactured in the United States of America

OPERATION: McMURDO SOUND

PROLOGUE

Winter was coming to Antarctica. By two P.M. it was already getting dark, and very soon the long night would descend upon the most inhospitable place on earth.

One hundred miles down the coast from the still active International Geophysical Year installations around McMurdo Sound and the Ross Sea, the weather was closing in. Beneath the lowering, overcast sky, temperatures were falling well below forty degrees below zero, and the wind was starting to kick up the snow atop the icecap.

No animal moved across the barren snowscape; no plants bent with the wind; and even the lowly lichens had shriveled and died for the season. For that moment nothing but the blowing snow moved, and there was no sound except for the howling wind.

In the graying dusk, however, a small speck of black appeared against the absolutely white background. It was lost in the blowing snow, and then reappeared, much closer this time, moving over the icecap at at least twenty miles per hour.

Soon, a deep-throated whine rose in volume even over the sound of the wind, and a large snowtrack, with an enclosed cab and a sled behind it, appeared over a hill of solid ice and then stopped, its engine idling.

A man inside the cab hunched over the steering column, and with a thickly gloved hand scraped away some of the ice from the inside of the windshield, trying to peer through the gloom. But then he shook his head, and his eyes went back to the dial of the homing instrument he had been trusting for the last hundred miles.

He was a large man, made even larger by the bulky clothing he wore. He pulled off the glove from his right hand, then with a blunt finger impatiently tapped the glass face of the instrument. The needle jiggled, but then settled back to the neutral position.

The instrument was useless. Broken. It hadn't been working now for the past fifty miles. And here, so close to the magnetic South Pole, near the Mertz Glacjer Tongue, a compass was totally useless.

Shaking his head in wordless frustration, the husky man yanked on his thick mitten, then pulled his snow goggles over his eyes, opened the door of the cab, and stepped outside.

The shrieking wind tore at his body, and it was with great difficulty that he trudged through the snow back to the cargo sled where he checked the lashings on the twenty-five gas canisters he was carrying.

He shivered when he was finished, not from the cold, but from fear, then trudged back to the cab of the snow-track where he got out a pair of nitrogen filled binoculars and scanned the bleak, forbidding horizon for a landmark. For anything recognizable.

At first he could see nothing except the windblown horizon, but then in the distance, to his relative south, he thought he could see a dark smudge. A jagged dark peak rising out of the snow.

Excited now, he ducked back into the cab and spread out a map. He looked out the windscreen a moment, then back at the map. It was Mt. Levich. Which meant he was more than halfway to the Oates Coast, and his rendezvous. More than halfway! He wasn't lost.

But he was worried. Before he had left, the meteorologists had warned that there was a better than fifty-fifty chance that the first of the antarctic winter storms would be developing along his route.

It looked as if he was heading for the wrong side of the odds, and if a full-fledged antarctic blizzard developed before he reached the relative safety of the coast, and the shelter waiting for him there, he would be a goner. There would be no chance of rescue. No chance of escape. He would be dead.

He shoved the map aside, slammed the snowtrack in gear, and continued down the coast, the deeply rutted tracks he left behind beginning to fill in as fast as he left them.

There was no turning around and going back. Only forward. Only forward . . . he kept repeating the phrase in his mind. Forward. Forward.

A little more than an hour later he was lost and he knew it. Darkness had come and the swirling snow was so deep that it made absolutely no difference whether he drove with the headlights or without them. There was nothing to see in any event.

He stopped, nevertheless, and tried to open the door of the cab to step outside, but now the wind was so strong he could not, and the snowtrack was being buffeted, rocked on its springs.

"Winds in excess of one hundred and sixty kilometers per hours," the meteorologist had predicted in his prim, precise manner.

If he tried to step outside he would become lost, and freeze to death. If he remained in the snowtrack with the engine running, sitting here in this spot, even the overhead exhaust pipe would clog with snow and he would die of carbon monoxide poisoning. And if he continued blind like this, there was a very good possibility that he would drive into a crevasse.

Two certainties, and one possibility.

He again put the snowtrack in gear, and continued in a direction that he thought was down the coast, but actually curved toward the South Pole. His thoughts alternated between the deadly cargo he was hauling, and of his wife and two children back home in their apartment.

Six months. He had only six months to go on this hellish assignment and he would be home after four long years.

He was frightened. He had been frightened all along, but now for the first time he consciously admitted it to himself. He glanced down at the snowtrack's speedometer needle which was bouncing above the thirty mark. He was driving too fast for good conditions, but insanely fast for the zero visibility conditions he was faced with now. And yet his foot pressed harder on the accelerator.

It would be autumn when he returned home, and the children would be in school. But that wouldn't matter. He had spent many hours with his friends, discussing exactly what he was going to do when he finally got home.

He was going to take the kids out of school for at least four weeks, maybe more. To hell with their lessons. They had a lifetime to catch up on them. He and his wife and the children were going south to lie on the beach and enjoy the warm weather. They would swim, and perhaps sail in a little boat. Mostly they were going to enjoy the two most wonderful things on this earth . . . laughter and warmth.

The snowtrack's speedometer needle was pegged now

at fifty, and the motion in the cab was violent, as the lumbering machine careered over the rock hard ice hummocks out of control for all intents and purposes. And the wind raged on, peaking at times to two hundred kilometers per hour. It was a full-fledged antarctic storm.

Just before the front skis of the snowtrack hit the opening over the crevasse, the man knew that he was not going to make it. And then the front of the machine lurched forward and down, and the man screamed in abject terror as the snowtrack and the heavily loaded sled it was hauling plunged into the wide crack in the ice, tumbling end over end.

The man struck his head against the plastic windscreen, starring it, and the control column jabbed into his chest, breaking three of his ribs.

Twisting as it fell, the machine slammed down on its side, the impact breaking the man's left arm and twisting his right leg out of its hip socket, and still the machine tumbled and fell.

The man screamed in pain and terror the instant the snowtrack slammed upright on its treads at the bottom of the fifty-foot-deep crevasse, driving his spine upwards, breaking it in several places. The heavily laden sled with its cargo of canisters came tumbling down on top of him, the hammering clatter filling his ears.

Then there was a silence in the man's ears, although he was still vaguely conscious.

It was all over now. A part of his mind knew that he was a dead man. There was nothing he could do about it. And yet some basic instinct for survival made him want to try . . . made him want to make the attempt to escape. He desperately wanted to see his wife and children again. Hear them laugh. Feel the warmth.

The storm was far above him now. The wind way in the distance. But another sound began to intrude on his consciousness. Outside. To his right, and slightly above him.

Somehow, the man managed to turn his head to the right—and he looked up. In the dim reflected light from his still-functioning headlights, he could see one of the small, steel pressure tanks, lying on the crumpled hood of the snowtrack. A hissing noise came from the canister; it was leaking.

With a burst of inhuman strength, the man managed to move; to actually edge a few inches away from the leaking canister.

Death, the single, horrifying thought crrystallized in his mind before his eyes glazed over. And then his throat began to swell; the nerves throughout his entire body began to thrum like a guitar string. He went totally berserk, his body thrashing and jerking uncontrollably, his broken spine ripping and severing key blood vessels, muscles, and nerves; his broken ribs punctured his lungs in half a dozen places; and at last, his tongue protruding from his chattering mouth, he bit completely through it, the blood pumping out, almost instantly freezing in the unbelievably cold antarctic temperature, while above, the storm raged.

CHAPTER ONE

It was spring, the best of all seasons in Washington, D.C. The cherry blossoms were lovely, the breezes were almost balmy, and the city had an expectant air about it.

Thirty days ago I had come in from a troublesome assignment in Europe, had taken one of the first uninterrupted vacations in my career, and now I was ready for some action.

David Hawk, the hardbitten director of AXE, had telephoned me last night at my apartment just after I had flown in from California, and asked me to come up to his office first thing in the morning.

It was a few minutes before eight A.M. as I swung my Alfa Romeo coupe around DuPont Circle and parked in the basement garage of Amalgamated Press and Wire Services, the front for AXE, and took the elevator up to the fifth floor.

For a full month I surfed, sailed, swam, and snorkeled in the clear Pacific waters, and generally bored myself almost to tears. Vacations were nice, but it was good to be back.

Hawk's secretary greeted me as I got off the elevator and told me to go right in.

David Hawk was an older man—just what his exact

age was none of us on the staff ever knew—short, in excellent condition, with a thick shock of white hair, and wide, intelligent, and very penetrating eyes.

I had seldom if ever seen him without a cigar in his mouth, and this morning was no exception. Hawk removed the cigar from his mouth, got to his feet and extended his hand as I crossed the room. We shook hands, his grip pleasantly hard.

"Welcome back, Nick," he said in his gruff voice.

"It's good to be home," I said.

He motioned me toward a chair, and when we were both seated, he looked critically at me for several long seconds.

"You look fit," he said.

"I am, sir."

"Ready to get back to work?"

I nodded. "Actually I was getting restless, doing nothing."

"You've soaked up enough sun and warmth?"

"Enough to last a while, sir," I said. "Is there an assignment?"

He nodded, and seemed to think for a moment. "This one may possibly be nothing more than a routine looksee, but it won't be pleasant."

"I see, sir," I said, although I didn't. But I have learned from long experience that Hawk is never to be rushed, and he never sends his people out on frivolous assignments. Whatever it was he wanted me to look into would be important.

"Give me your gun," Hawk said, and he hit the intercom button. "Has Mr. Kerchefski come up yet?"

"He's here now, sir," his secretary replied.

"Send him in."

I had pulled out my 9mm Luger from its shoulder holster, removed the clip, and handed them both over to

Hawk. A moment later the door opened and Spaso Kerchefski, AXE's brilliant, but somewhat eccentric armorer, came in.

The man wordlessly crossed the office, nodded at me, and took my Luger and clip from Hawk, held it up to his nose and then shook his head. "This will never do," he said.

"Will he need another weapon?" Hawk asked.

I was about to protest—my Luger was like an extension of my own body—but Kerchefski chuckled. "This piece is admittedly crude, but I will be able to fix it. Graphite instead of oil, and some of the springs and smaller slides will have to be replaced."

"I want it by noon."

"Of course," Kerchefski said, and he turned on his heel and left the office with my Luger.

When we were alone again, Hawk grinned, which was a rare expression for him. "Every chance the man gets he tries to convince me to get you to update your weaponry."

I returned the smile. "I'd be lost without the Luger. It's a bit on the heavy side, but it's quick, reasonably accurate, and I know it."

"What do you know about Antarctica?" Hawk asked, the sudden change in topic startling, but typical of his approach.

"It's cold, the seasons are reversed, and at least eleven different countries, including ours, maintain scientific stations there."

Hawk was nodding. "Ours is operated about half and half by the Navy and by civilians. The Russians about the same."

"Yes, sir," I said.

Hawk pulled a file from a stack, opened it, shuffled through the papers, then closed the file and handed it across to me. "You can look through this on the way down."

"Sir?"

"You're going to McMurdo Sound on the Antarctic continent."

"What's the trouble down there, sir?" I asked. I had always thought Antarctica was the only peaceful continent on earth. No weapons. No fighting soldiers. Nothing but research.

"Maybe nothing in this, but I want you to look around just the same," Hawk said. He sat back in his chair, and relit his cigar as he marshaled his thoughts. "Our Navy maintains a number of different installations on the continent. Most of them are on or around McMurdo Sound itself, but there are a number of research stations inland, closer to the pole. Radio contact was lost with one of these inland installations seventy-two hours ago."

"I would expect that would not be too unusual, sir," I said. "Considering the terribly harsh climate down there."

"Under ordinary circumstances I'd agree with you. Really nothing to worry about, and certainly nothing for us to concern ourselves with."

"But?"

"I spoke with the President yesterday. He met with me and the chairman of the Joint Chiefs to express his concern. Wanted to know what we could and should do."

I had a sudden premonition that this was going to be far less than "routine," but I held my silence, and Hawk continued.

"We're in a delicate position here, Nick. The installation is about a hundred miles inland from Mt. Levich, very isolated and not talked about very much."

"I would assume everyone on Antarctica knows about the place. It would be hard to hide with so few people down there."

"Everyone knows about the installation, but not about its true purpose."

"Which is?"

"Genetic research."

"Sir?"

"Military research in genetic engineering. The Russians are way ahead of us on this one. And believe me, Nick, if the Russians weren't mucking about in the field, we'd drop it. They're working on new diseases, and we're working just as hard on universal antidotes."

"Why Antarctica?" I asked.

"Because if there is an accident—an outbreak they call it—the isolation and harsh climate would minimize the effects."

"Outbreak?" I asked. I could envision a number of very unpleasant possibilities. We had all been to school on that one.

"Biological accidents anywhere else in the world could endanger all human life. It's not work that we're proud of, but it's necessary I'm told."

This one was going to be complicated, and already I wasn't liking it. But I suspected that Hawk was going to tell me much more—none of it pleasant.

He sighed. "Thirty-six hours ago, during a break in the weather, a helicopter with a pilot and one crewman was sent out from McMurdo Sound to the camp. Their instructions were simply to fly over at low altitude and visually survey the installation. Nothing more."

I could almost envision the bleak, harsh landscape, the helicopter appearing at the horizon, and then hovering overhead.

"At first they could see nothing," Hawk continued.

"What I mean to say is that everything seemed normal. Although there was no movement, nothing seemed to be out of the ordinary."

"So they landed."

Hawk nodded, grim lipped. "They landed all right, but within two minutes the crewman was on the radio, frantically screaming for help. And then nothing."

"On an open radio channel?"

Hawk nodded again. "Another helicopter was sent out, this time with strict instructions not to land. Only to take photographs."

Hawk opened another file and extracted several photographs, passing them across to me. The pictures showed a bleak, forbidding landscape indeed, with dark huts jutting up from the stark white background. There was radio antennae, a generator building, a fuel dump, supplies, barracks interconnected with laboratories and a common room. A typical arctic or antarctic installation. But there was a body near the door of the common room building, another near one of two helicopters.

"The man by the door is the pilot, the one by the helicopter is the crewman. Dead," Hawk said.

I looked up at him. "Everyone heard the message from the helicopter?"

Hawk nodded. "They're all clamoring for an explanation. They demand to know whether there is some kind of trouble out there that everyone should know about."

"Is there?" I asked softly.

"I honestly don't know. Neither does the President. No one knows. But it's gotten to the U.N."

"We'll be in trouble, won't we, if the kind of research we've been doing is discovered."

"No," Hawk said. "Everyone else down there is doing the same thing. I'm told that the things we're doing are clearly for defense. Antidotes only."

"Then what killed them?"

Hawk passed a hand across his eyes. "We don't know. An accident? Sabotage? It's anyone's guess."

"My guess," I said.

"In part. Under pressure from the U.N., the President has agreed to an international commission of scientists and doctors to go out and investigate. I want you down there, Nick. If there's any mess to clean up, or any of our secrets to be secured at that camp, you're the man for the job."

I had a sour taste in my mouth for this one, and I told Hawk so.

"I agree," he said. "But we're way out on a limb. We've got to make sure what happened. You'll be doing more than securing the site. You'll be keeping your eyes and ears open, so that you can come back and provide us with a totally unbiased report. We just don't know what happened down there."

I reached inside my jacket pocket, took out a cigarette and lit it. I inhaled deeply. "When do I leave?"

"This afternoon. San Francisco, Australia, New Zealand, and then Victoria Land . . . McMurdo Sea."

"My cover?"

"You'll be a genetic scientist. It'll take the better part of two days to get you there. You'll be accompanied by an expert in the field who'll brief you extensively, then be a part of the American team."

"What has the scientist been told about me?"

"You're Captain Nick Carter, a special investigator for the Navy. Your contact at McMurdo Sound will be the special commission leader, Navy Commander John Tibert. A good man."

"He believes I'm Navy as well?"

Hawk nodded, and for a moment we both were silent.

"What do you think happened down there, sir?" I finally asked.

Hawk took a second or two to answer me. "They had

an accident, I suspect," he said. "Unfortunate, but they all understood the risks."

I got to my feet.

"You can spend the rest of the morning here," Hawk said. "Your flight to San Francisco leaves at two this afternoon."

"Where do I meet the scientist?"

"She'll pick you up in California, before your flight down."

"She?" I asked.

"The best in the field, from what I'm told."

"Yes, sir," I said, liking this even less. But it was useless to argue with Hawk, and I didn't even try.

"Good luck, Nick, and be careful."

"Yes, sir," I replied, and I left his office taking the case file with me, and went immediately down to my own office in Operations.

For the remainder of the morning I buried myself in the file Hawk had provided me with, which included information not only on the research installation, but on the scientists who had worked there, and were now presumably dead.

Later, I pulled what information our files contained on Antarctica, its development, the nations manning research stations there, as well as the continent's terrain and weather.

Not an inviting place. In fact from my reading I gathered that Antarctica was probably the most harsh and forbidding place on this planet. And now there was trouble there. Somehow, deep in my gut, I had a feeling that whatever had happened at the research station was going to turn out to be more than a simple biological accident. But I had absolutely nothing on which to base that feeling at the moment. Nothing more than a hunch.

Around noon, Kerchefski came up to my office with Wilhelmina.

"I've replaced the oil with graphite and beefed up some of the more delicate mechanisms," he said. "With temperatures in the range of fifty and sixty below zero, this weapon would never have functioned. The oil would have stiffened up, and the strain on the smaller parts would have broken them."

"Thanks," I said.

Kerchefski looked at me for a long moment. "When you return I'd like to sit down with you and talk about a new choice of weapons."

"Sure," I said, but I had absolutely no intention of doing any such thing. I think he knew it.

He shook his head, sighed theatrically, and left my office.

I cleared up some last minute business, hurried back to my apartment where I packed a few things, secured my weapons in my specially built radio-cassette player so I could bring them through airport security, and then ordered a cab for the airport.

It was just coming into spring here in Washington, the weather warm and lovely. At McMurdo Sound, however, it was coming into the long Antarctic winter. Not a pleasant place to be.

Dr. Lana Edwards turned out to be a lovely woman in her early thirties. Her hair was cropped short, her eyes were wide and dark, her face tiny and delicate, and her body small and compact.

She met me at the airport in San Francisco, and after we had introduced ourselves, she led me across the mezzanine to the cocktail lounge.

"We have a couple of hours before our international flight leaves, Captain," she said. "We might just as well make use of the time to get to know each other."

"We're going to be working closely together for some time," I said. "Call me Nick."

We went into the bar and sat down at one of the tables. She didn't smile.

"I'd prefer Captain Carter," she said.

I raised my eyebrows.

"The Navy has no business doing what it is doing down there," she said. She had a lovely accent.

"Canadian?" I asked.

She just looked at me for a long moment, but finally she nodded. "I was born in Canada. But I'm an American citizen now."

"A pacifist?"

Again she nodded. "And you're a hawk."

I had to laugh out loud, although I wasn't too happy about the situation. She was definitely going to make things difficult.

The waitress came, and I ordered a brandy on the rocks. Lana ordered a ginger ale.

She definitely was going to make things difficult.

CHAPTER TWO

We landed at Auckland on New Zealand's North Island about two in the morning after a grueling twenty-hour flight from San Francisco.

From there we took a small commuter airline flight down to the city of Dunedin on South Island, where we were met by Navy Lieutenant Joe Zipco.

"Welcome to Down Under," he said after he had helped us through customs. He was young, probably in his mid-twenties, and he seemed to have a perpetual smile.

"What's the program, Lieutenant?" I asked. "Dr. Edwards and I are a bit tired."

"You can call me Mailman, sir, everyone else does."

"Mailman?"

He smiled and nodded. "Zipco sorta sounds like zip code, you know. So they hung Mailman on me."

I had to laugh despite my exhaustion, but Lana Edwards was having none of it. She was what is known as a "tight-assed broad."

"I'll require a shower, a hot meal, and a bed, Lieutenant," she snapped as we left the terminal building and climbed into the back seat of a Navy staff car.

Mailman looked back at us, then shook his head.

"Best I can offer, ma'am, is a flight seat on the transport aircraft, a bumpy ride, and a box lunch."

Lana started to protest, but I cut her off. "We're leaving immediately?"

"Yes, sir. The aircraft is waiting across the field. We have a window on the weather pattern, and if we don't go now, we might not get in for a few weeks."

"How are the box lunches?" I asked.

"Terrible," he said grinning. He started the car, pulled away from the terminal building, and headed across the field at breakneck speed.

I glanced over at Lana, seated next to me, but she was staring out the window, apparently lost in her own dour thoughts. She had not loosened up at all during the long flight down from San Francisco. In fact the longer we were together, the more uptight she seemed to become. I had no idea what her problem was, but I resolved that if and when her attitude began to get in the way of our investigation I was going to bounce her little ass off the project.

The last of a pile of supplies was being loaded through the belly doors of a Hercules C130 transport aircraft sitting on the apron in front of a large hangar. The plane had U.S. Navy markings on its tail and fuselage, but most of the several dozen personnel servicing it wore civilian clothes.

"An early winter this year, sir," Mailman said. "We were sorta caught with our pants down as far as resupplying our installations on the Sound goes."

"I'm not riding in that thing," Lana protested.

Mailman looked at her in the rearview mirror. "Sorry ma'am, but it's the only way down at the moment. But it's up to you."

"I'll ride with the Soviet delegation . . ." she started to say, but I cut her off.

"Belay that," I snapped. I looked at Mailman's image in the mirror. "You didn't hear a thing."

"It's the wind," he said. "Affects my hearing something awful."

A man in a Navy uniform, his parka open, broke away from a group loading the aircraft when we pulled around, and he came over to us when Mailman parked near the belly doors.

"Captain Carter?" he said as I climbed out of the back seat.

"Right," I said, and we saluted, then shook hands.

"Lieutenant Ridley. I'll be flying this crate."

Lana had gotten out of the car, and she came around to us. He turned to her.

"Dr. Edwards?" he said, extending his hand.

She ignored it. "I'll have to make a telephone call before we leave."

"Sorry, Doctor, that won't be possible. We're leaving immediately," Ridley said.

"I *will* make the call," she said, her eyes flashing.

"I'll send you a postcard," I snapped, and I took Ridley's arm, and guided him to the aircraft. "Tell me about your box lunches," I said. "Mailman says they're world famous."

Ridley laughed, and we walked up the ramp into the plane, then worked our way forward and past the last of the crates being strapped down—without bothering to look back.

A couple of jumpseats had been installed just behind the navigator's position on the wide flight deck, and Ridley motioned to one of them.

"I'll round up my crew and we'll get out of here," he said, as I sat down and buckled myself in.

He left, and a moment later Lana appeared through the hatch, and without a word took her place in the other seat and strapped herself in.

For a minute I debated saying anything to her, but decided that if she was going to tag along, I would have to set her straight.

I leaned a little closer to her, and she flinched as if she thought I was going to attack her.

"One thing before we take off, Lana," I said softly. "You were presumably briefed back in California. You know that all twenty-seven of the installation's people are probably dead, along with the helicopter pilot and his crewman. You also know the nature of the work that was being done there. And finally you are aware that we're not going to be alone on this mission, despite its sensitive nature to our government."

She held her silence, but there was a play of emotions across her pretty face.

"If you step out of line one more time, if you even give so much as a hint that you're about to step out of line, I'll kick your pretty ass up around your shoulders, and then send you home."

She colored slightly.

"Have I made myself clear?"

She glared at me for a moment longer, but then turned away as Ridley and two other men clambered onto the flight deck.

"Mailman you know. He's our navigator on this little milk run, and the ugly one is Tom Tubbs, my co-pilot," Ridley said climbing into the left seat.

"Captain Carter," Tubbs said, shaking my hand.

"Nick."

"My friends call me Tubby," he said, grinning. He climbed into the right seat, completely ignoring Lana.

Mailman climbed into the navigator's position, put on his earphones, and then his fingers danced over the controls on the sloping panel over his head.

"Sharp left at the stop sign, and then straight out Broadway past the post office," he quipped.

"Gotcha," Ridley said, and one by one the C130's engines whined into life.

Mailman turned to me again. "Two thousand miles to the Sound . . . a little less than seven hours. If you want something to eat, the coffee urn is just around the corner, and next to it are the lunches."

"Thanks," I said. "But I think I'm going to try for a little sleep."

Tubbs turned around. "If you can sleep on this run, I'll personally buy you a steak dinner and all the beer you can drink at the club."

"You're on, Tubby," I said, closing my eyes, and within five minutes after we had lifted off I was asleep.

I actually dozed, off and on, for about four hours, until I finally opened my eyes, stretched, and unbuckled my seat belt.

"Sleeping beauty is awake," Mailman said, and Tubbs turned around to look at me. He shook his head.

"I'll take my steak medium rare," I said.

"You were faking, weren't you?"

"Nope."

"Shit," Tubbs said, and the others laughed. Lana wasn't in her seat.

"Where did she run off to?" I asked.

"Powder room," Mailman said.

I nodded. "Any reason I can't smoke."

"Go ahead," Ridley said. "And get yourself a cup of coffee right away. In about twenty minutes you won't have the chance to drink it."

I got up and came forward so that I could look out the windshield. Far below us the dark sea was studded with huge icebergs, but directly ahead of us a seemingly impenetrable dark gray wall rose up from the water and towered well above our flight altitude.

"Looks a little rough out there," I said.

"It'll be a hell of a ride," Ridley said.

"Any chance of us having to turn back?"

Ridley looked around at me. "How important is it that you two get there?"

"Very."

He nodded. "Then drink your coffee now, we'll be in the shit in about fifteen minutes or so."

I turned, ducked through the hatch, and stepped out into the galley area. Lana was leaning against the bulkhead, a cup of hot coffee cradled in her hands. Her eyes were wide, her complexion white, and a thin bead of sweat had formed on her upper lip. She looked up.

"Are you all right?" I asked.

She shook her head. "I'm frightened."

"You can stay at the Sound," I said. "You don't have to come out to the installation with us."

"No, not of that, I've never been on an airplane before in my life."

"Oh Christ," I said, understanding suddenly dawning on me.

"They said something about a storm," she said. Her lower lip was quivering. She was on the verge of tears.

All the while on the long flight down from San Francisco she had been uptight. But it hadn't anything to do with me. She had simply been frightened out of her mind about flying. I hadn't realized.

"Drink your coffee," I said, "and then we'll have to go forward and strap ourselves in. It's going to be a little bumpy."

"Oh God . . ." she said.

"Take it easy, Lana. Those guys up there are pros. They do this all the time. We'll be all right."

She wanted to believe me, I could see that. But I could also see that she wasn't going to make it in one piece.

"Hang on a second," I said, and I went back onto the flight deck and quickly explained the problem to Ridley.

"Tranquilizers are in the first-aid kit," he said.

Mailman got them out for me, gave me a couple of the pills, and I brought them back to her. "Take these, it'll help," I said.

She did as I told her, and by the time I had a quick smoke and half a cup of coffee, a dreamy look was beginning to come into her eyes.

I took her coffee cup and threw it in the trash receptacle, then took her by the elbow and started to lead her back to the flight deck when the plane lurched into an air pocket. She was thrown against me, and for just a second she tried to struggle away, but then it was as if she had melted, and she pressed her body against mine, her arms around my neck.

"Hold me, Nick," she said huskily. "God . . . hold me." She turned her face up to mine and closed her eyes.

I kissed her, long and deep, and she pressed harder against me until the plane lurched again.

"You two better strap in," Ridley shouted from the flight deck.

"Right," I said, parting from Lana, and I helped her forward where I strapped her in her seat, and then strapped myself in.

Outside there was nothing to see now except for a white, swirling mass as the C130 plowed its way through the antarctic storm. All the time Lana Edwards stared at me, a stupid grin on her face.

The American installation at McMurdo Sound was a sprawling complex of rambling huts, radio towers, satellite dishes, and supply dumps. In any direction, for as

far as the eye could see, there was nothing but a waste-
land of snow and ice. Huge drifts were piled everywhere
in the camp, and as we came in for a landing we could
see that the runway had evidently just been cleared.
Throughout the camp, personnel were digging out after
the fierce storm that we had encountered.

Although it was only two in the afternoon, it was already twilight, when the Hercules touched down, rolled
to the end of the runway, and then turned and taxied
back to the administration and supply area. There were
no buildings anywhere on the base large enough to
hangar the aircraft, so we stopped out in the open.

"Too much wind to put up anything more than a one-
story building down here," Ridley explained. "The aver-
age year-round wind velocity is around fifty miles per
hour. During storms we've clocked steady winds—not
gusts—at more than a hundred miles per hour. Sometimes it's a real chore just to keep the heavily guyed radio towers up."

The Hercules turned majestically, then came to a halt.
A moment later Ridley and Tubbs hit a series of
switches and the engines whined down to a halt.

"Welcome to Antarctica," Ridley said, unstrapping
and climbing out of the pilot's seat.

"Once again I've made it without getting lost,"
Mailman said.

"Dumb luck," Tubbs quipped, and everyone but
Lana laughed. She was still feeling the effects of the
tranquilizers I had been steadily feeding her during the
flight through the storm.

I unbuckled her seatbelt and then helped her to her
feet as Ridley went aft. He came back a few seconds
later with thick boots, heavy parkas, and thick mittens.

"Better put these on," he said to us.

I glanced out the windscreen. The entrance to the

nearest building was less than a hundred yards away.

Ridley grinned. "You can try it if you want, Nick, but it's sixty-three degrees below zero out there at the moment."

I took the clothing from him without a word, helped Lana pull hers on, and then got dressed myself, as Ridley, Tubbs, and Mailman donned their cold-weather gear. When we were ready, the rear cargo doors opened, and we shuffled outside, the air so cold it took my breath away.

Heavily dressed ground personnel were moving in to unload the plane as we headed across to the administration building, and by the time we made it to the door my cheeks stung, my eyes and nose were running, and my legs were numb with the unbelievably intense cold.

The installation nurse, one of the few females on the base, took charge of Lana. Ridley and his crewmen went off to file their reports, and I was shown in to Commander John Tibert's office.

Tibert was a bull of a man, six-feet-four, at least two hundred and fifty pounds, with thick dark hair, a swarthy complexion, and a heavy black beard with only a few flecks of gray in it.

His tiny office was crammed with books, maps, and posters of bikini-clad girls on sunny Florida beaches.

After our introductions, I pulled off my parka and sat down across the desk from him. As I lit myself a cigarette, he poured us both a healthy measure of whiskey and then he too sat down.

"Cheers," he said, raising his glass. He didn't seem happy.

I raised my glass in salute and we drank.

"Dr. Edwards had a rough time of it, I'm told," he said.

"She's afraid of flying. We put her on tranquilizers."

"Will she be all right?"

I shrugged. "When do we leave for the installation?"

"Tomorrow sometime. The other commission members have reached their bases. They'll be shuttling over here this afternoon. We'll have our briefing first thing in the morning, and then get started."

"What happened out there, Commander?" I asked.

"Paul," he said. "I wish the hell I knew, but there's just no way we're going to be able to second guess it without actually going out to the site ourselves."

"Tough luck about your helicopter pilot and crewman."

"Tough luck all the way around," Tibert said. "Have you been told who the other commission members are going to be?"

I shook my head. "It hadn't been worked out before I left."

"Besides the usual crowd, we're going to have a Russian, a Chinese Communist, and an East German. It's going to be one hell of a show."

I sat forward, took the whiskey bottle, and poured us both another drink. "You know what my job is, Paul," I said. "I'm going to need your help."

"You've got it."

"What was going on out there?"

"Genetic research—" he started to say, but I interrupted him.

"I mean what was *really* going on out there? What don't we want the Eastern Bloc people to know about?"

"That's the hell of it, Nick. Nothing was going on that we're ashamed of. We were working on antidotes for biological warfare agents."

"Were they working with anything potentially dangerous?"

"As far as we were aware of, no."

I hesitated a moment before I asked my next question. "About the twenty-seven people out there. Any of them with an axe to grind? Any of them off on their own tangent?"

Tibert hesitated a moment also before he answered. "I'd like to give you an unqualified no on that one as well, but I can't. It's the one factor that has me most worried." He paused, and I held my silence. "Living down here puts a strain on everyone. The constant wind. The harsh weather. The storms. The primitive conditions. You can't hop in your car and go for a little drive, or walk through the woods. Ping-Pong in the rec hall will entertain the troops just so long before they start to break apart."

It was the answer I had expected. The one variable factor in this entire mess that would make my job difficult.

"What else could have happened out there?" I asked, changing my tack. "Sabotage?"

"Not likely," Tibert said. "We may all be a little crackers down here, but by and large we're a pretty peaceful bunch. Conditions are just too goddamned tough to be playing games like that."

I finished my second drink.

"Another?" Tibert asked.

"Not now," I said. "I'm tired. Point me to a bunk if you would. I have a feeling that the next few days are going to be busy."

"And miserable," Tibert said, getting to his feet.

Most of the buildings on the base were connected by unheated corridors called antarctic tunnels. Tibert showed me around the complex. I was issued the cold weather gear I'd be needing, I was fed a reasonably good meal in the mess hall, and then was shown to my room, a tiny cubicle with a cot, a dresser, and a small closet.

One tiny window looked out on the forbidding land-scape.

"Dr. Edwards is in the next room down," Tibert said. "She's sleeping."

"Thanks," I said tiredly. The cot with its thick, quilted blanket suddenly looked very inviting.

"If you decide to get up in the middle of the night for a stroll, I'd just as soon that you didn't go outside. You'd probably freeze to death."

"Don't worry," I said. "I'll be staying put."

After Tibert left, I checked on Lana. She was sound asleep. Then I went back to my room, got undressed, and crawled into bed, falling asleep the moment my head hit the pillow.

CHAPTER THREE

The wind was moaning outside around the edges of the buildings when something woke me up. For a long time I lay there listening to the lonely, forsaken sound, my senses alert for something else.

I raised my left arm in front of my face. The luminous dials on the watch read a few minutes after two in the morning. Just about everyone at the installation would be asleep, except perhaps the radio people, and one or two scientists working on overnight experiments.

Then I heard an out-of-place sound, and I sat up, shoving the covers aside. It sounded like whimpering. Or crying. As if some kind of animal were in pain.

I got out of bed, the floor ice cold to my bare feet, grabbed my Luger from under my pillow, and then stood stock still, listening for the sound.

It came again—from Lana's room. I moved across the room to the wall and listened. It was Lana, and it sounded as if she were crying.

I let out the deep breath I had been holding. I had been a little jumpy ever since Tibert had told me who was going to be on the commission. It was my natural, in-born distrust and suspicion, I suppose, but it had made sleep difficult and had caused me to awaken with Lana's crying.

My feelings for the woman had vacillated between anger and pity. She was obviously having a tough time of it down here, but if she was going to work with the commission on this assignment, she was going to have to pull herself together before we met with the others and went out to the installation.

I stuffed my Luger back under my pillow, went to the door and opened it a crack. There was no one in the corridor; it was so cold I could see my breath.

For a moment I thought about putting on some boots, but then shrugged. I was only going to be a minute or two, just long enough to find out what the hell was wrong with her now, calm her down, and then come back to bed. We were all going to need our sleep.

I stepped out into the corridor and went down to her door, then put my ear to it. I could hear her whimpering, and I was just about to knock, when I heard another sound, and I froze.

There was someone else in the room with her. I had heard a voice, soft and indistinct, but loud enough for me to recognize it as a man's. Not Lana's.

For a moment I debated slipping back to my room for my gun, but then decided against it. There was no telling what was happening here.

I took a deep breath, held it a moment, then tried the doorknob. It was not locked.

Carefully I turned the knob all the way to the right, then slammed the door open, leaped into the dark room, and side stepped to the right.

"Help," Lana's muffled shout came from the bed.

The silhouette of a large man, dressed in cold weather gear, leaped up from the bed and came at me as I charged him.

"Nick," Lana shouted, as something slammed into the back of my head, causing my knees to go momentarily weak.

I watched helplessly as the man in front of me drew back his fist and slammed it into my face, and I started to fall. I grabbed out at my attacker, got a fist full of the front of his parka, and then went down heavily.

It couldn't have been more than a couple of seconds later that Lana was helping me to my feet, but it had been enough time for the two men to make it out of the room and down the corridor.

I staggered to the door and looked out just as the antarctic door at the end of the corridor slammed shut, and then everything was quiet again.

"Are you hurt?" Lana asked from behind me.

I stood there staring at the outer door for a long moment as everything began to come back into focus. The back of my head hurt, and my jaw was sore. But I'd live.

After a while I turned around, flipped on the light, and closed the door.

Lana was dressed in a long flannel nightgown, a wide frightened look in her eyes, and her complexion stark white except for a large red mark on her left cheek.

"What happened here?" I asked.

She shook her head. "I don't know . . . I don't know," she said, her voice trembling. "I woke up with one of them holding my mouth."

"What'd they want?"

She looked beyond me to the door. "They asked about . . . about you. They wanted to know what you were doing here?"

"Me, by name?" I asked, stepping toward her.

She nodded. "They thought I was a Navy investigator, too. They wanted to know how long we had worked together, and what we knew."

"What'd you tell them?"

"Nothing," she said. "I was too frightened to speak. Then one of them hit me."

"You didn't say a thing to them?"

She shook her head. "You came in a second later."
I tried to think this out.

"Are you all right?" Lana asked.

I looked up at her and managed a slight smile. "I've got a hard head," I said. "What did they look like?"

"It was too dark. I couldn't see their faces."

"How about their accents? Russian? Chinese? German?"

She shook her head. "I don't know, Nick. Only one of them spoke, I think. And he was whispering. I was too frightened to tell . . ." She let it trail off.

Between us, on the floor, I noticed a large, black button. I stepped forward, bent down and picked it up. "Yours?" I asked.

She looked at it. "No," she said.

There was no insignia on the button, like the buttons on our Navy uniforms. But I was fairly certain that I had pulled it off the parka of the man who had hit me in the face as I went down. It wasn't much, but it was something.

Obviously someone from the commission, who knew that I would be included on the team going out to the installation, wanted to know more about me. Wanted to know just how much I knew, and exactly who I was. Which meant someone on the commission was worried about me. Which also meant that whoever it was, had something to hide. But that could have been anyone—including our own people. Commander Tibert had said that the one variable factor in this entire thing was the effect the isolation down here had on the scientists.

A renegade working on his or her own little project? Something that had killed the entire installation out there? An experiment that had backfired, and now someone wanted it covered up—even from their own government?

They were all possibilities.

"I don't want you to say anything about this to anyone," I said, pocketing the button.

"But . . . they could have killed you, Nick," Lana said.

"Could have, but they didn't," I said. "They were looking for information, that's all. But I don't want you to say anything about it."

"Commander Tibert will have to be told."

I shook my head. "No one."

She turned away and ran her fingers through her hair. "What's going on down here, for God's sake?"

I went to her, and she turned around and came into my arms. "I don't know," I said gently. "But that's what I was sent down to find out. And if I'm going to do my job, it's going to have to be my way. Agreed?"

She looked up into my eyes. "Agreed," she said after a moment, and then her lips parted slightly, and she closed her eyes.

I kissed her, and almost immediately she pressed her body against mine.

"Don't go, Nick. Stay here with me."

"They're not coming back," I said.

"I don't want to be alone," she said huskily. "Please stay."

"The hawk and the dove?"

She had to smile at that. "Not a bad combination," she said. She stepped back away from me, and before I could do a thing, she had gathered up the hem of her nightgown, pulled it up over her head, and then tossed it aside.

Her body was small and compact, her breasts well formed, the nipples hard, and the small tuft of pubic hair a light blonde.

She turned, went to the bed and crawled in beneath

the covers. "Don't just stand there," she said. "Turn off the lights and come to bed. It's cold in here."

I hesitated for a moment, but then shrugged. It *was* cold sleeping alone. I flipped off the light switch, got undressed, and crawled into the narrow bed with her, and she came immediately to me, kissing my face and neck, as she moved her body against mine.

After we made love, we slept for a couple of hours. Around six-thirty A.M., we both took a shower in the bathroom at the end of the corridor, got dressed in the cold weather gear we had been issued, then went together down to the busy dining hall across from Administration.

The large room was busy, and after Lana and I had gotten our trays of food from the line, Tibert waved us over to where he was seated at the head of a long table.

There were a half dozen people seated with him, a woman among them.

"This is Captain Nick Carter, and Dr. Lana Edwards," Tibert said rising. "They'll be a part of the team."

The others nodded their greetings.

"I'll make more complete introductions later this morning at the briefing," Tibert said, as Lana and I sat down.

We ate our breakfast in silence, tension obvious not only around our table, but throughout the entire room. Something terrible had happened out at the installation. Everyone knew about it, and everyone seemed to be holding their breath awaiting the outcome of our investigation.

An hour after we had sat down, Tibert pushed his coffee cup aside and got to his feet. "Ladies and gentlemen, if you will follow me now, we'll go to the briefing room and get started. I want to be ready to leave for the site no later than noon."

There were murmurs of assent, and we all got to our feet and followed Commander Tibert out of the dining hall, through Administration, and down another long, unheated corridor to a large room set up with a long table around which were ten chairs.

Tibert took his place at the head of the table, and everyone sat down, Lana and I to Tibert's right.

"Please smoke if you wish. There are notepads and pencils here if you would like to take notes, and the equipment and supplies each of you brought along are being loaded aboard the helicopters at this moment," Tibert began.

"What has happened out there at the site?" the woman seated at the other end of the table asked.

"We'll get to that in just a few minutes, Dr. de Hoorn," Tibert said. "First, I think introductions are in order. Then I shall brief you on the situation as it exists at this moment, and finally we will try to come to an agreement as to exactly how we're going to handle this investigation."

"While your people have time to clean up the mess?" one of the men said from the end of the table.

"The site has not been disturbed by us, or by anyone else," Tibert said. "I assure you."

No one else said a thing, and Tibert began his introductions with Lana, and then me, identifying us both as genetic scientists.

I got to my feet before Tibert could proceed. Someone already knew that I wasn't a scientist—probably someone on this committee—and I felt that everyone else should have the same advantage.

"As far as anyone outside of the room is concerned, I am what Commander Tibert said I am. But for your information, I am not a scientist. I am a U.S. Navy investigator."

There were several murmurs of protest around the table, but I held up my hand to silence them.

"An accident of some sort evidently happened at one of our research installations. I have been sent down to find out exactly what happened. That is only natural. You, on the other hand, have been included in *my* investigation because Antarctica is international domain. What happens down here could affect all of our countries. But this has been structured as, and will remain, an investigation of a U.S. installation."

I sat down. Some of the people around the table seemed pleased by my admission, while others seemed upset.

Tibert looked at me for a long, appraising moment, and then continued with the introductions.

Included around the table were Dr. Boris Stalnov, a Soviet genetic scientist; Dr. Henri Jean Père, a French chemist; Dr. Donald Bates-Wilcox, a British microbiologist; Dr. Elsie de Hoorn, a Dutch physician; Dr. Kim Tien Sing, a Chinese Communist physician; Dr. Kurt Abel, a West German geneticist, and his exact counterpart from East Germany, Dr. Peter Straub.

There were ten of us, including Tibert and myself, representing eight nations and four different scientific disciplines.

It was a very mixed group, and already I could see several different factions beginning to form. There would be trouble among them. Everyone could see it.

"I wish to register a protest," Stalnov said. "This is an international scientific inquiry. A U.S. Naval investigator has no business being included."

"Your protest is noted, Dr. Stalnov."

"Well?"

"Well what, Doctor?"

"What are you going to do about it, Commander?"

"Not a thing, Doctor," Tibert said. "Now, may we proceed?"

No one else said a thing, and Tibert began his briefing, which contained essentially the same information that Hawk had given me. The only exclusion was that Tibert did not mention the fact that we were aware of the Soviet's work on biological warfare materials here on the Antarctic continent. His explanation of our installation's work was that our scientists were doing harmless genetic experiments.

"Harmless, you say," the Russian snapped. "Then what killed your people?"

"That's what this commission will determine, Doctor," Tibert said patiently.

"Then let's get on with it!"

"We will," Tibert said. "First, are there any questions about the situation as we know it at this moment?"

"Have any other fly-overs been ordered?" Bates-Wilcox, the British microbiologist, asked.

"Weather permitting, every four hours around the clock."

"Any sign of life whatsoever?" Bates-Wilcox asked.

"None," Tibert said.

"Have air samples been taken?" Jean Père, the Frenchman, asked.

"We thought it too risky at this stage, Doctor."

Some of the others started to protest, but Lana sat forward.

"Commander Tibert is correct in his caution," she said. They all turned toward her. "From what we've been told, the helicopter pilot and his crewman died within minutes of their touching down at the installation. If their deaths are attributable to an airborne agent, the act of gathering the agent could prove fatal to the collection aircraft's crew."

"Preposterous," Dr. de Hoorn spoke up.

"On the contrary, Doctor," Lana insisted. "Our first task, as I see it, will be to approach the installation with extreme caution. We'll wear biological safe suits. I'll go in with the leader helicopter to make an air sample test. If it's all clear I'll signal."

"Then I will accompany you," Dr. de Hoorn said.

Lana nodded, and sat back.

"Other questions or suggestions?" Tibert asked.

"A procedure must be established here and now," Stalnov said.

"Right," Tibert said dryly. "Once the all-clear has been given, we will enter the camp. Our first job will be to reactivate the normal life support systems. Heat, water, lights, food, radio contact. I've made out a tentative duty roster for those jobs."

There were no objections.

"Once we've settled in then, we will all work together on . . . ah . . . body collection," Tibert said. A silence descended. "We're assuming that whatever killed our people out there worked fast. So fast that no radio messages could be sent. If that is the case, then there will be bodies at the various duty stations. They'll have to be photographed, their exact location and posture noted, and then carried to a central area."

Still no one said a thing.

"A pathology laboratory will have to be set up then. I would suggest they be staffed by our two physicians, Dr. de Hoorn and Dr. Tien Sing, as well as one of our geneticists, and perhaps our microbiologist, Dr. Bates-Wilcox."

"I will act as the pathologist geneticist," the East German, Peter Straub said.

Tibert nodded.

"And the rest of us?" Lana asked.

"Our approach will be, of course, at least partially

determined by the findings of pathology, but it will be our job to track down the source of whatever it was that killed our people out there."

"So much for the scientists," Stalnov said. "What about you and Captain Carter? What will you be doing all the while?"

"Whatever is necessary, including keeping the peace," I snapped.

Stalnov smiled. "Perhaps the most difficult job of all."

The meeting broke up a couple of hours later after a lot of technical talk between the scientists, most of it speculation as to the kinds of biological agents that could have killed the installation's scientists, and then remained active long enough to kill the helicopter pilot and his crewman.

We were instructed to gather our personal equipment and assemble back at the Administration building within one hour for immediate departure by helicopter out to the installation.

Lana and I stayed back, and after the others had left, Tibert got up. "What do you think, Nick?" he asked.

"Stalnov was right," I said. "It's going to be a major job just keeping the peace between them."

"Not much we can do about it," Tibert said. "The commission stays as is."

"Stalnov is no scientist," Lana blurted.

We both turned to her. "What?" I asked.

"Stalnov. The Russian. If he's a geneticist, then I'm the fairy godmother."

"Are you sure, Lana?"

"Reasonably sure," she said. "He doesn't know what he's talking about. Dr. Abel, I think, picked it up, but Straub, the East German, covered it up."

"Oh Christ," Tibert said. "Just what we need."

"Boris Stalnov is a genetic scientist. But he's an old man. At first I thought this Stalnov might have been his son. But he's not."

"I'll have to get an okay from Washington, but I'm not having the man on this commission," Tibert said. "He's probably a KGB officer."

"Leave it be," I said.

"I can't . . ." Tibert started to protest, but I held him off.

"Hear me out, Paul," I said. "If Stalnov is KGB, and as long as he doesn't suspect we're aware of it, he could be a big help."

"How?"

"If it wasn't an accident out there, but sabotage, and if it was a Soviet plot, Stalnov will be out there trying to cover it up. I'll keep an eye on him." I looked at Lana who obviously wasn't liking this at all. "It just may be that Stalnov, or whoever he really is, will lead us to whatever happened out there."

"It's too dangerous, Nick," Lana said.

"She's right," Tibert said. "A lot of innocent people could get hurt."

"I think a lot of innocent people have already been hurt, Paul. It's up to us to find out what the hell really happened out there."

Tibert was having trouble with it. "On your responsibility?"

I nodded.

Tibert sighed deeply, then looked at his watch. "Get your gear. I'll see about the helicopters and the weather."

Lana and I left the meeting room and went back to our quarters.

"Why didn't you tell him about what happened last night?" she asked.

"Because Tibert's an administrator, a peacetime officer. If I told him what happened he would have called off the investigation."

"I'm not so sure that wouldn't be for the best, Nick."

"We might never find out what happened out there."

"I'm scared, Nick," Lana said at my door.

"Stay here then," I said.

She thought about it a moment, but then shook her head. "No," she said. "We'll figure out what happened out there together."

"The dove and the hawk?"

"The scientist and the cop."

CHAPTER FOUR

Although it was only a few minutes past noon, it was dusk already, the sun very low on the horizon. In a few more weeks it would be dark twenty-four hours a day down here, until the antarctic spring finally came in October.

The wind blew the snow in long, jagged plumes off the roof peaks and around the lamp posts as the ten of us trudged away from the Administration building and across to where two helicopters were waiting, their rotors slowly revolving.

We all wore biological safe suits over our cold weather gear, although we carried the air tanks and helmets. Those we would put on as we approached the installation.

Lana and the Dutch physician de Hoorn got in the lead helicopter, while the rest of us piled into the second machine.

Tibert and I sat just behind the pilot and co-pilot, and after we were strapped down, we lifted off in a flurry of snow from the downdraft of the rotors.

We were going to shadow the lead helicopter by ten miles, hanging back until Lana and Dr. de Hoorn radioed us the all-clear.

As we rose I could see the Ross Ice Shelf and McMurdo Sound itself, the American camp spread out in a haphazard fashion. Inland, however, there was nothing but the jagged ice hummocks, and the pure white snow that seemed to stretch on forever.

The lead machine banked sharply to the right, gained a little altitude, and then flashed away inland for the one hundred mile trip out to the research installation.

I glanced back at the others, but none of them looked up. They were all engrossed in their own thoughts. Some of them were sorry that this had happened, others were smug that it had happened to the Americans and not to their own people, while at least one of them—I was sure —knew more about what had happened out there than the rest of us. Last night's attack on Lana proved that.

A few minutes later our helicopter surged forward with a burst of speed, and the communications radio blared.

"Unit one, this is two, we're ten miles out and matching speed," our pilot said.

"Roger unit two, ETA forty-two minutes."

Tibert leaned forward, tapped the pilot on the shoulder, and took the microphone from him.

"Unit one, this is Commander Tibert. I want you all to put on your helmets and hook up to your air cylinders at ten miles out. Is that an affirmative?"

"That's a roger, Commander," the pilot of the lead machine radioed back.

"I don't want you to take any chances," Tibert said. "Drop the ladies off and then get out of there. Return immediately to base camp."

There was a silence on the radio.

"Is that an affirmative unit one?"

"Hold on a second, Commander, I think I see something."

"What is it?" Tibert spoke into the mike.

"Something was moving down there . . . I thought," the pilot radioed. "Do you want us to turn around for a look-see?"

"Negative, negative," Tibert snapped. "Proceed to the installation."

"Roger."

"And keep us posted, Chip."

"Sure thing, Commander."

Tibert gave the microphone back to the pilot, then swiveled around in his seat so that he could look out one of the side windows down at the bleak landscape beneath us.

"What'd he see down there, Paul?" I asked softly.

"I don't know," Tibert said without turning around. "Probably nothing. Under these lighting conditions, with the wind and the shadows, probably nothing."

"We don't have anything down there?"

"Not a thing, Nick," Tibert said looking at me, and then at the others who were all watching us. "Nothing should be moving down there. We've got some weather coming in no later than twenty-four hours from now. No one else should be down there."

No one said a thing, and Tibert turned back to the window and continued to study the terrain. But the light was fading fast now, and it would be dark within a few minutes.

I unzippered my bio suit and parka and pulled out a cigarette. It was possible, I thought, that an accident had happened at the installation, killing everyone there. The Russians, doing their own research with biological warfare agents, would naturally be extremely interested in what had gone on.

If that was the case, then they would have to suspect that I had been sent down here to cover up.

I had to smile inwardly. Pick a fact and build a scenario around it. The typical policeman's mentality. But in this business there were more possibilities than facts.

About a half hour later, the radio blared again.

"Unit two, this is one, at ten miles out and holding."

"Roger unit one," our pilot radioed, and our helicopter slowed and hovered five hundred feet above the ice and snow while we waited for the people in the lead helicopter to don their helmets and seal their safe suits.

A couple of minutes later, the unit one pilot was back on the air.

"We're ready, Commander."

Our pilot looked back, and Tibert nodded.

"Unit one, proceed," the pilot radioed. "We're right behind you."

"Roger."

Our helicopter surged forward again through the night, all of us with our own strained thoughts about what we would find when we finally got there.

A few minutes later the lead unit pilot was back on the air.

"We've got the installation in sight now," the speaker blared.

Tibert took the mike from our pilot. "All right, Chip, I want you to be careful. If it looks bad down there, if you get spooked, anything, I want you to get the hell out of there, understood?"

"Roger."

"All right. Give us some chatter now. I want to know what's going on."

"We're down to about two hundred feet. I'm going to hover here for a couple of minutes. Dr. Edwards wants to take an air sample."

Our pilot slowed his machine down, and he too hovered, but ten miles out from the installation.

"How far are you from the camp?" Tibert radioed.

"About two hundred yards," the radio blared. "Dr. Edwards has the air sample. Wait a moment."

There were no sounds except for the helicopter's engine and the slight hiss from the radio, until Lana came on the air.

"Looks clean at this point," she radioed.

Straub, the East German, sat forward. "Ask Dr. Edwards how deep she's gone with her particulates filter."

Tibert relayed the question.

"One part per billion," Lana radioed immediately. "I put it in the heaters and ran a carbon dioxide test as well. Everything is clean."

Tibert looked back at Straub, who nodded after a moment.

"All right, Chip, at your discretion you can move in a little closer."

"Roger. I'm going to set it down right in front of the main building."

There was another couple of minutes of silence until Lana was back.

"We're on the ground, about twenty yards from the main building. The air tests clean."

"What do you think?" Tibert asked, glancing back at the others.

Straub nodded. "Proceed to the building itself. Near the . . . ah . . . body of the pilot."

Tibert turned back to the radio. "All right, Dr. Edwards. I want you and Dr. de Hoorn to unload your equipment so that my pilot can get out of there. That is if you judge the situation there to be safe."

"I'm going to take one more air sample near the building," Lana said.

"Roger," Tibert said. "Chip, as soon as she gives the

all-clear and they unload their equipment, I want you to get out of there.''

"That's affirmative, Commander.''

We waited then, again in silence, for a few minutes.

"She's coming back . . . no she's motioning for Dr. de Hoorn,'' the unit one pilot radioed.

"What's going on out there, Chip,'' Tibert snapped.

"I don't know, sir. Hold on a sec.''

Tibert glanced at me, worry etched deeply around his eyes.

"They're doing something to Al . . . to the body by the door,'' the pilot said. "I can't see what's happening. Wait. They're coming back now.''

Tibert was nervous, and the tension amongst the other commission members was thick.

"It's all clear here,'' Lana radioed. "We're unloading now. You can come in.''

"Stay out of the building, Dr. Edwards. Do not go inside until we arrive.''

"We'll wait,'' Lana said.

Tibert motioned for our pilot to go ahead, and our machine surged into the night as I searched out the forward windows for lights of the other machine.

"They're unloaded now, Commander, and I'm lifting off,'' the pilot of the lead machine radioed.

Then I could see the lights rising out of the darkness ahead as we approached the camp.

"Got you on visual, Chip,'' our pilot radioed. "I'm coming in low.''

"Good luck,'' Chip said, and we watched as the other helicopter rose even higher and then flashed overhead on its way back to the base camp on the Sound.

We came in low and slow, touching down twenty yards from the Administration building, where we could see Lana and Dr. de Hoorn doing something to the body by the door.

"Put your helmets on now, and start your air supply," Tibert said, turning to the others.

"The air tests have shown negative," Stalnov protested, but the rest of us pulled on our helmets and adjusted the air flow from our tanks. A moment later so did Stalnov.

When we were ready, Tibert opened the main side doors, and within a couple of minutes we had quickly unloaded our equipment, and the helicopter lifted up into the sky, banked to the left, and headed back to base camp.

"Does everyone copy," Tibert's voice came through the tiny speaker in my helmet.

I touched my throat mike beneath my suit. "Loud and clear," I said. And everyone else answered in the affirmative, as we all trudged over to the building where Lana and Dr. de Hoorn were still bent over the body of the dead pilot.

The man's eyes were open, his face fixed in a permanent death mask of fear, a lot of blood on his chin.

Lana looked up and shook her head.

"What killed him?" I asked. "Any preliminary guesses?"

Dr. de Hoorn looked up at me. "I don't know yet," she said in a subdued voice. "But the man bit completely through his tongue, his spine is broken in at least three places, and half the muscles in his body have been ripped and torn."

"Good Lord," someone said softly.

Lana and de Hoorn got stiffly to their feet.

"That's not all, Nick," Lana said. "He was . . . shot too."

She bent down again, and turned the body over on its stomach. There was a small hole in the back of his parka, a small amount of blood around it.

I glanced back at the helicopters behind us. I could

just see the shape of the crewman who had radioed for help.

"Check the air inside the building," I said, turning back. "Paul, check out the generators to see if they're still working. We can't stay out here all day."

Lana and Tibert nodded.

"Dr. de Hoorn, come with me," I said, and I turned, brushed past the others standing there in a little group, and strode across to the helicopters.

The crewman was in much the same shape as the pilot. He was sitting on the snow, his back against the machine's skids. In one hand he held a microphone, in his other a military .45 automatic. His eyes were open, his face screwed up into a grimace, and there was a lot of blood on his chin and down the front of his parka. He had also bitten through his tongue.

Dr. de Hoorn had joined me. We looked at each other.

"I want to know if the same thing that killed the pilot killed this man," I said.

"No way of knowing that for sure, Captain, until we perform an autopsy."

"I need your best guess," I insisted.

She shrugged and went to work on the dead crewman, unzipping his parka and feeling at his back, then his shoulders and arms. When she was finished she got up.

"The massive injuries are similar. The tongue, the broken spine, the torn muscles."

"What could have caused it?"

Again she shrugged. "Nerve gas, any of a couple of dozen chemicals or drugs."

"A biological substance?" I asked.

She stepped a little closer to me, as if she could tell me her answer in private, although everyone could hear us.

"With genetic engineering at its present level, there could be an unlimited number of agents that could have done this, Captain Carter. Is that the answer you were looking for?"

"Yes it was," I said. I bent down, pried the .45 from the dead man's grasp, clicked the safety on, and pocketed the gun.

"Oh God," Lana's voice came through my helmet speaker.

"What is it?" I shouted, looking toward the Administration building. The others stood there by the open door.

"Jesus," Lana said.

I raced toward the building, Dr. de Hoorn directly behind me. "Get the hell out of there, Lana," I shouted as I ran.

Reaching the entryway, I roughly shoved Stalnov and Straub out of the way, and stepped inside.

The main room was large and dark except for the beam of Lana's flashlight, which jerked this way and that from where she stood a few feet away from me.

I took my flashlight out, flipped it on, and surveyed the mass destruction in the common room.

There was blood and bodies everywhere. A woman, or what looked like a woman's body, lay sprawled over a table, a fire axe through the back of her head. Three bodies were crumpled in a heap by the couch, their faces frozen in horrible expressions of pain and shock, blood down their chins from where they had bitten through their tongues. The doorway that evidently led into one of the antarctic corridors was clogged with at least a half dozen bodies, one of them partially unclothed. And in the far corner, near a book rack were two men, their hands around each others throats, lying where they had died.

I moved over to where Lana stood. "Have you taken an air sample?" I asked.

She turned her head to look up at me, her eyes wide

behind the face plate of her helmet. "What in God's name happened here?"

"That's what we've come to find out," I said. "Have you taken an air sample?"

She shook her head.

Straub, the East German scientist, had come in, and he took the air testing unit from Lana, opened the outer airlock, and then ran the two experiments.

A minute or two later he was finished, and he looked over at me. "The air is fine," he said, his German accent thick.

"Are you sure, Doctor?" I asked.

"As sure as I can be," he said. He slowly unclasped his helmet, cracked the seal, and then took it off, and breathed deeply of the air inside the room.

I reached up to undo my own helmet but he motioned me to wait, and I hesitated.

"Give it a couple of minutes, Captain," he said from his throat mike. "If anything is to happen to me, it will happen within that time."

"How do you feel?" I asked.

Someone else swore, and I glanced behind me at the door as the others came into the room.

"Cold, nothing more," Straub said.

"Where's Commander Tibert?" I asked, searching the faces, but not finding his.

"He went to check on the generators, as you asked him to," Jean Père, the French chemist said.

A second later the lights flickered once, twice, and then the third time they came on.

"Bloody hell," the Britisher, Bates-Wilcox, said. And some of the others muttered something, and others gasped.

"The air is safe, I think," Straub said.

I looked at him, then slowly unclasped the catches on

my helmet, cracked the seals, and lifted it off. The air was bitter cold, but had absolutely no smell to it.

Something clicked behind me, and to the left, and a warm blast of air began. The heaters had come on with the electricity.

Dr. de Hoorn had taken off her helmet, and she too noticed that the heat had come on. "We're going to have to get these bodies outside before they thaw out," she said. "Otherwise we're going to have troubles."

Tibert had come to the door and he stepped inside, then stopped, his eyes wide, his nostrils flaring, as he surveyed the death and destruction.

"You heard the lady," I said after a moment. "Let's get these bodies outside."

"Wait," Tibert interjected. "We've got to take photographs."

"Is it necessary, Paul?" I asked.

He nodded. "If we're going to have any chance of finding out what happened here, what really happened here, we're going to have to do this right."

"I think it's fairly obvious what happened here," Stalnov said.

Tibert spun on his heel, yanked a .45 automatic from his bio suit pocket, and was on Stalnov in two steps, pressing the barrel against the Russian's temple.

"One more word, you sonofabitch, one more, and I'll splatter your fucking brains all over this room!"

"Paul!" I shouted.

The Russian was holding stock still. Tibert was shaking so badly I was afraid he would fire by mistake.

"Paul, not this way!" I shouted again. "Back off!"

Slowly, Tibert stepped back, lowered the .45, and uncocked it.

Stalnov started to say something, but I shook my head.

"No one says a word," I snapped. "We're going to get these bodies outside before they thaw out, and then we're going to search for the others. When we've got them all outside, we're going to clean up this mess and then figure out what our next move will be."

No one said a thing.

"Who is going to act as photographer?" I asked.

"I will," the West German, Kurt Abel said. He went outside to the packs, and was back a few minutes later with a 35mm camera and strobe unit.

Then for the next hour we stacked the bodies outside to the left of the main door in a ragged row, until we had all twenty-seven of them laid out, along with the helicopter pilot and crewman.

The West German was good. As unobtrusively as possible he worked slightly ahead of the rest of us, photographing each of the bodies at least once, some of them more than once.

When we were finished with that grisly task, we all worked as a team, no one complaining, to clean up the incredible mess that had been left behind, finally finishing a few minutes after six P.M.

Lana and Bates-Wilcox had put on the coffee and made some soup and sandwiches after running tests on the water and food. Tibert had found the installation commander's liquor locker, and had broken out a couple of bottles of brandy.

The main building, which contained the day room, the dining hall and kitchen, a few offices, a supply room, and the radio and meteorology room, was warm enough by the time we had finished so that we were able to take off our bulky outer clothing and sit around in comfort.

We had all gathered in the dining hall for the makeshift meal, when Tibert announced that he had made radio contact with the main camp.

"Did you tell them the situation out here?" I asked. Everyone was looking down the table at Tibert.

He nodded. "I gave them a preliminary report," he said. "We'll set up the pathology lab in the supply room of this building and begin right away this evening."

"Aren't there laboratories on this base?" Straub asked.

"Yes there are," Tibert said tiredly. "But we don't know for sure yet if whatever killed these people came from those labs or not. Until we determine that, we're going to confine most of our activities to this building."

No one said a thing, and Tibert continued.

"De Hoorn, Tien Sing, Straub, and Bates-Wilcox will set up and run the autopsies. The rest of us will work through this installation room by room. I want every single item in this camp tested and catalogued."

"That could take days," Stalnov said.

"Yes," Tibert replied tiredly. "Any other questions?"

There were none.

"Then finish your meal. The sooner we get started, the sooner we'll be finished and be able to call for a ride out of here."

CHAPTER FIVE

The dining hall became the central clearing house for what Tibert was calling our "search and define" mission. A pathology lab had been set up in the supply room, and tissue, blood, and bone samples had already been taken from the first three bodies. Although no results had come from the tests as yet, Lana and Dr. de Hoorn were confident that by morning they would have an answer for what killed everyone here.

The rest of us had begun working room by room through the installation: checking the heater ducts, the water and sewage systems, the personal effects of the scientists and technicians who had worked here, and the piles of supplies that had been stored for the long winter.

We worked in teams of three and four, often returning to the dining hall for coffee or food and to compare notes.

Stalnov, as it turned out, was proving to be an invaluable investigator (which I suspected in reality he was), discovering a well hidden bag of marijuana in one of the rooms, and in another a scientific journal, which outlined how the scientist had manipulated experimental results to fit his own pet theories.

This last find Tibert confiscated over Stalnov's protests.

"I'll allow Drs. Straub and Abel to examine the journal once I've looked through it," Tibert said. "If, in their opinion, there could be something in it that has a bearing on our investigation, I will release it for everyone's information. Until that time, however, it is the property of the U.S. Government."

Stalnov had been mollified, somewhat too easily I thought, by that proposal, and we had continued our work into the night, while outside the wind continued to build.

I had been working with Jean Père and the West German, Kurt Abel, for most of the evening, and it was around two in the morning when we went back to the dining hall. Stalnov and Lana were there, at opposite sides of the room, having coffee and a sandwich.

"Find anything?" Lana asked tiredly.

I shook my head, then went across to the coffee urn where I poured myself a cup, adding a little of the brandy to it. I brought my coffee back to the table, and sat down across from her.

"You look beat," I said.

"I am," she said. "And discouraged. I just came from talking with Elsie and Dr. Tien Sing."

"Anything from them yet?"

She shook her head. "Dr. Straub is running the main-line tests, but it'll be hours before he comes up with anything . . . if he ever does."

"Something killed these people," I said.

"Obviously. But it may have been a self-destructive organism."

"What are you saying?" I asked.

Jean Père and Dr. Abel had been standing nearby, and the West German spoke up.

"What Dr. Edwards is saying, Captain Carter, is that whatever killed these people may have been absorbed into their bodies, and then dissipated, leaving behind no traces."

"Then we may never know what killed them?" I asked.

"Not quite," Jean Père said. "If a man is found stabbed to death, we can still make a fair approximation of the type and size of the murder weapon, by its effects."

"But we've found nothing here, so far, that could have caused those effects," I said.

"That is correct," Abel said. He yawned and put his coffee cup down. "It has been a long, trying day. I am going to get some sleep."

"An excellent idea," Jean Père said, and the two of them left the dining hall.

I leaned forward toward Dr. Edwards. "Have you seen Paul this evening?"

"He was here a little while ago," she said, indifferently.

"Did he say where he was going?"

She shook her head, but then looked up. "I think he said something about checking the fuel supply for the electric generator."

I looked at her for a long moment. "Are you sure?"

"No," she said impatiently. She got to her feet. "I'm going to bed."

"I'll walk you back," I said getting up.

Together we left the dining hall, then down the antarctic corridor to a block of rooms we had cleaned out earlier for our own use.

We stopped at her door. "Don't come in, Nick," she said. "I'm tired."

"Me too," I said kissing her chastely on the cheek. "Get some sleep, I'll wake you in the morning."

She nodded, and went into her room. As soon as her

door was closed, I hurried back to my own room, pulled on my cold weather gear, then slipped back out into the corridor, and out one of the exit doors.

It was bitterly cold outside, and the wind had risen dramatically since we had arrived, snow blowing everywhere, making visibility almost impossible.

From what I remembered of the camp layout-diagrams I had seen, the generator building was just across from the Administration building, next to the radio antenna. It was less than a hundred yards from this cluster of buildings, but in these conditions the distance was nearly impossible.

Hunched forward against the biting wind, I worked my way along the corridor until I came to the Administration building. The windows were lit up, and although they were frosted over, I could make out the shape of someone moving around inside. It was probably Stalnov, or one of the scientists from the pathology lab.

I looked out into the blowing snow, trying to catch a glimpse of the radio antenna or one of the lights on top of the generator building. But I could see nothing; the darkness was too intense.

There was a path from the front door of the Administration building to the generator building. If I could find it I might be able to make it across. But I was going to have to be careful out here. It would be very easy to get lost in this weather.

I edged farther around the building, until, just a foot or two from the front door, I stumbled over something, and looked down.

It was a rope, half buried in the snow. I picked it up and followed it to its end, which was attached to the Administration building.

A guide line to the generator building? It was logical. The crew here would have found it necessary to check on the generator on a regular basis no matter what the weather. They would have had to string a guide line between the two buildings.

Holding the guide line at waist height with both hands, I stepped away from the Administration building and headed slowly out into the storm.

There was a path of sorts, although it was mostly covered over now by the blowing snow. From time to time I had to stop and dig the rope out before I could continue. There was nothing ahead but blackness, and once I stopped and looked back, but I could no longer see the lights of the Administration building behind me. I was alone in a cocoon of blowing snow.

What seemed like hours later, but was probably less than fifteen minutes, I was suddenly able to pick out the halo-like glow of a single light ahead of me.

I hurried forward, and ten yards later came to the front door of the generator building, the sounds of the diesel engine loud the moment I opened the door and stepped inside.

The building was fairly large. One of the generators bolted to the concrete floor was running, while the back-up unit next to it was silent.

When I had the door closed behind me, I unzipped my parka and pulled the hood off.

Although no one was here now, someone had come in not too long ago. A trail of melted snow led away from the door, around the spare generator, and ended at a large metal cabinet in one corner. I tried the handle, but it was locked.

Tibert had evidently been here, had checked something in the cabinet, and then had left. It was possible that the figure I had seen through the Administration building window was Tibert's. But what had he been doing out here?

I started to bend down to examine the lock when the handle clicked and the cabinet door swung open, bumping me on the head.

I jumped back reaching for my Luger, when Tibert stepped out of the cabinet.

When he saw me, his eyes went wide.

"Do you always hide in closets like that, Paul?" I asked, relaxing.

Tibert glanced over his shoulder, a guilty expression on his face. "I . . ."

"What have you got in there?" I asked. "Anything I should know about in case the others start asking questions?"

He sighed deeply. "You know everything else, you might just as well see this," he said. He shoved the door all the way open, then turned and went back inside. "Come on," he said.

I followed him into the cabinet where he was doing something with the back, next to a set of tools. A large section of the back wall opened inward to reveal a set of stairs leading downwards.

"Secret passageways and all," I said.

"Close the outer door. It locks automatically," Tibert said, and he disappeared down the stairs.

I did as he said, and followed him down the stairs, which descended at least twenty feet below the generator building.

At the bottom, Tibert flipped on a light in a tiny vestibule, punched out a code on a door lock next to a heavy metal door, and it swung open.

"During construction we dug out a wide, deep trench in the ice, built this section, then covered it over with steel plates, and finally snow. The generator building was constructed right on top of it," Tibert said.

He stepped inside, flipped on a light, and I followed him in.

It was a large room, and evidently once had been a laboratory of some kind. But now all the equipment was destroyed, glass beakers and chemicals broken and spilled everywhere.

Along one wall, a series of file cabinets were open, and I could see ashes in a couple of the lab sinks where at least some of the files had obviously been burned.

"Did you do this?" I asked, surveying the damage.

"I destroyed the files, yes," Tibert said.

"I mean everything else. All the damage."

Tibert hung his head. "Yes," he said. "I had to make it look like they went berserk down here, too. If the others discover this lab, I want them to suspect the same thing happened down here, as above."

I came farther into the room and headed across to the file cabinets.

"There's nothing left there," Tibert said.

I turned around. "What kind of work was being done down here, Paul?" I asked.

"Genetic engineering. The same as above."

"Then why was this place hidden? Even my people knew nothing about it."

Tibert sat down on one of the lab stools and lit himself a cigarette. "This place was built about ten years ago. Long before my time down here."

"This lab, or the entire installation above?"

"Both," Tibert said. "It was a civilian project—I forget just who—M.I.T., or perhaps Harvard. This was the isolation lab. It was at a time when the first of the real troubles over genetic manipulation were coming to the surface. From what I understand, the Navy knew about this place—unofficially—but we turned a blind eye to it."

"So what little concoctions were brewed up down here?"

"Nothing so far as I know. And that's the truth, Nick.

This lab was used for barely two years, and then it was considered superfluous, and it was closed down."

"Who reactivated it?"

"Me," Tibert said.

"Because of the Russians?" I asked. I found another lab stool and sat down across from Tibert.

He nodded. "We found out through Navy Intelligence that they were stepping up their genetic research on RVB-A substances, and—"

I interrupted him. "What's that?"

Tibert smiled, but the expression was grim. "Rapid Varying Bio-Agents," he said. "In the simplest terms, they're biological materials that can be introduced into a human body and produce a fatal illness. The key is their ability to rapidly change function. As soon as the body's natural immune system begins to attack the invading virus, the agent changes function."

"No antidote?"

Tibert shrugged. "That's what we were working on down here. As soon as an antidote was introduced, the RVB-A would change function on us. It was crazy."

"So there can be no defense."

"We don't know that yet," Tibert said defensively. "We were right on top of a breakthrough here. We were coming up with a counter RVB-A, that would change its antidotal function as fast as the invading RVB-A."

"And?" I asked. I was getting a fair idea now of what could have happened here.

"We hadn't come up with it," Tibert said. "We were at least a month away from it."

"That's not what I mean, Paul."

"What then?"

"In order to come up with an antidote, your people would need to have a supply of the RBV-A itself. Isn't that right?"

"Yes," Tibert said looking directly into my eyes.

"Some of it got loose then. There was an accident down here that killed everyone."

"No."

"How can you be sure, Paul?"

He sat forward. "The RBV-A we were using, every bit of it, carried low-grade nuclear tagging. We did that so that if there ever was an accident we could trace the bio-agent responsible."

"And you're saying now that traces of radioactivity would have been found in the bodies?"

"That's right," Tibert said. "But there was no trace. And what RVB-A we had on hand down here is intact. I destroyed it."

"No chance there was an untagged batch?"

"None," Tibert said. "None whatsoever."

There were only two possibilities then, I told myself. Either Tibert was lying to me now—which I didn't think he was—or we were back to square one; something outside this camp killed these people.

"What do you think happened here, Paul?" I asked.

"At first I thought it had been an accident with the RVB-A. But when there were no traces of the tagging element in any of the bodies, I came down here to check that there were no untagged samples. There were none." He looked away momentarily. "Someone killed them. They were murdered."

"Why and by whom?"

Tibert flared. "Jesus Christ, isn't it obvious? The Russians are working on the RVB-A material. They found out somehow that we were close to a breakthrough on the antidote, and they wanted to stop us. So they came out here and murdered everyone."

"How did they kill them?"

"Probably with an RVB-A."

"And it leaves no traces."

"None," Tibert said. "But I couldn't stop the formation of the commission. Not from down here."

"And now you intend killing Stalnov."

"It'll be an accident," Tibert said.

"Then we may never find out for sure, if it was the Russians," I said.

"It was—"

I held him off. "No. Listen to me, Paul. Now that we've come this far, let me take it from here. If it was the Russians, we have to know for sure."

"Why?"

"So we can stop them," I said.

"Impossible," Tibert snapped.

I ignored the comment. "Stalnov is no scientist. He was sent out here to find, and if possible, secure the antidote. Until he does that, his mission won't be complete."

"So we stop him, what then?"

"We're going to stop more than Stalnov," I said. "But he's the key. First we have to prove that the Russians actually killed your people here. Stalnov may provide us with that information. And secondly we're going to have to find out where the Russians are manufacturing their RVB-A."

"That last part is easy," Tibert said. "Their lab is about a hundred and fifty miles from here. Just up the Sound from our base camp."

"Has any of the RVB-A been shipped back to the Soviet Union?"

"I don't know. But I tend to doubt it. From what we've been able to gather, they've just come up with the stuff on an experimental basis. And in any event I don't think they'd risk shipping it by air. If there was an accident they'd kill a lot of people. They'd never be able to live through the repercussions."

"So they'd send it by ship."

Tibert nodded. "But we're passed the shipping season."

"Submarine?" I asked. "Could a submarine get through?"

Tibert thought a moment. "I suppose it could."

"Where?"

"Where what?"

"Where would the submarine come to pick up the material?"

"Anywhere along the coast . . " Tibert started to say, but then he stopped in mid-sentence. "No. They wouldn't come anywhere near the Sound, or even into the Ross Sea. There's too much air traffic."

"So they'd have to surface somewhere along the coast to the east or west of McMurdo Sound."

He looked at me for a long minute. "What are you getting at?"

"Have you got a map of McMurdo Sound and the coastline east and west?"

"Upstairs in Administration. There's a map on the wall in the office."

"Let's go take a look at it. I've got an idea," I said. It was only half formed, but based on what Tibert had told me, and on the probability that Stalnov was not a scientist, I felt it was worth pursuing.

"Do you mind telling me?"

"Let's look at a map first," I said.

Together we left the lab, went up the stairs and stepped out of the cabinet back into the noisy generator room. When Tibert had the door relocked, we zippered up our parkas, then went back outside.

The wind was even stronger than before, and it took us nearly twenty minutes to make it back to the Administration building.

Everyone had evidently gone to bed, because the day

room and dining hall were deserted. I went with Tibert
into the installation commander's office where we closed
the door and then flipped on the light.

A large map of the entire Antarctic continent was
tacked on the wall behind the commander's desk, and I
went immediately to it.

"Find me a ruler," I said. "Or some kind of straight
edge."

Tibert rummaged through the desk and cabinets,
coming up with a yardstick, which he brought over to
me.

Marked on the map were the various installations
around McMurdo Sound, as well as this place.

I laid the yardstick on the map, one end of it at the
Soviet's main base, and swung the other end in an arc
toward the coast to the east. The line from the Soviet
base to the coast near the Mertz Glacier Tongue passed
within fifty miles of this installation.

Tibert finally saw what I was doing, and he shook his
head. "It's too far," he said.

I looked at him.

"If they had been transporting the material to a
submarine rendezvous on the coast, and there had been
an accident, it would not have affected this installation."

"How close would they have had to come?"

Tibert shrugged. "Ten miles. Maybe fifteen. It's hard
to tell."

I looked again at the line I had drawn on the map.
Ten or fifteen miles. But the closest the line came was
fifty miles. Still, I wondered, could something have happened out there? Something to make the transport vehicle come closer?

"It's no good," Tibert said. "There would have been
no reason for them to come any closer than the fifty
miles."

"What if they got lost?" I asked. I was clutching at straws, I knew. But it seemed to fit so well.

"They'd have homing devices to guide them."

"How about sending a flight out to find out."

"Even if it would do any good, nothing is flying in this weather."

"I want you to radio the base camp and order a coastal surveillance. If there's a Russian sub out there, I want to know about it."

"All right," Tibert said after a moment's hesitation. "I'm not going to send the message in the clear, however. I'll encode it, and send it within the hour. But the weather people were predicting that this storm could last as long as several days. The flight will have to wait until then."

"Do what you can, Paul," I said. I was suddenly tired. "I'm going to get some sleep, I think."

"Good idea. As soon as I get the message off, I'll go to bed as well."

CHAPTER SIX

I lay in bed for almost two hours, and although I was tired, sleep wouldn't come. I kept thinking about the things that Tibert had told me. If the Russians had indeed developed the biological warfare agent Tibert had described, and if they managed to transport a supply of it back to the Soviet Union before we came up with the antidote, we would be in very great trouble.

Visions of New York City filled with dead people kept marching across my mind's eye, until at last I got out of bed and got dressed.

I was going to have to get a message off to Hawk, alerting him of the possibility that a Soviet submarine could be leaving these waters with a highly deadly cargo.

The radio and meteorology room was just off the installation commander's office. The equipment was all on and humming, but Tibert wasn't there. He had probably sent his message ordering the air surveillance as soon as the weather cleared, and then had gone to bed. But I thought it was a little odd that he had not turned off the radio gear.

I went across to the equipment. On the table in front of the transceiver was a clipboard containing a brief message, in code. Tibert's message. But why had he left it here, out in the open? It didn't make sense.

I turned the volume up on the receiver, but only static came from the speaker. The equipment seemed to be working properly at this end, there were just no signals.

I scraped some of the frost from the window and tried to peer outside toward the antenna tower. The storm was still going strong, however, and I couldn't make out a thing.

It was possible that there was some kind of antenna trouble and Tibert had gone out to check. But I wondered. I had a strange feeling about this.

I tore off Tibert's message sheet and stuffed it in my pocket as I hurriedly checked the dayroom and dining hall. No one was there, nor was anyone in the pathology lab. Everyone was presumably in bed asleep.

The corridor in the living quarters was quiet as I put my ear to Tibert's door, then knocked softly. There was no answer, and after a moment I opened the door.

Tibert wasn't there, and his bed hadn't been slept in. His parka was missing too.

I went down to my room, grabbed my parka and put it on as I went back down the corridor to the day room and then outside.

The wind was shrieking now, at least fifty or sixty miles per hour, the snow blowing so thickly that it was impossible to see more than one or two feet ahead.

Just outside the doorway I groped around in the snow until I found the guide line that led the hundred yards out to the generator building and the radio tower.

But this was insanity. Even if something had malfunctioned with the radio antenna I couldn't see how Tibert expected to find the trouble and then fix it in this weather.

Holding tightly onto the rope I stepped out and away from the building, a gust of wind knocking me to my knees, almost causing me to lose my grip on the life line.

Then, with my head bent low, I crawled on my hands and knees away from the Administration building, my world reduced for that time to the wind, the snow, and the incredible cold that penetrated even my antarctic gear.

It took at least half an hour to make it the hundred yards, although I had no idea how far I had come until my head bumped into the side of the generator building and I looked up.

Carefully I got to my feet, let go of the rope, and, trailing one hand against the wall of the building, worked my way to the door, opened it, and stepped inside.

The generator was still running, but there was no fresh snow on the floor. Tibert had not been here again.

I remained in the heated building for a few minutes, then opened the door and stepped back outside.

The radio tower rose fifty feet into the sky just around the corner from the door. I worked my way along the front wall, and at the corner stepped around into the full fury of the wind. I was almost knocked off my feet again, but this time I regained my balance more quickly, and, bent low, I stumbled forward, using the building as a guide.

Thirty feet away I came at last to the base of the radio tower. I looked up. There were no lights visible, and at first I thought I wasn't seeing the red beacons because of the storm, but then I realized that something was wrong, drastically wrong.

I grabbed one of the tower rungs and started climbing upwards. Less than five feet up, even before I came to the roofline of the generator building, the tower ended in four, twisted steel stubs. The tower was down.

Quickly I climbed back down, and dropping to my

hands and knees, I crawled away from the building, coming within a few feet to a twisted section of the tower.

Following the bent steel girders outwards, away from the building, I came to a pair of guy wires twisted around on themselves. Sitting in the snow I hauled the wires in, hand over hand, until I came to the end of them.

I pulled my flashlight out of my pocket and in its dim light I examined the ends of the guy wires. They had been cut. The ends were not twisted and frayed. They were straight and smooth.

I looked up. Someone had come out here and cut the guy wires. Someone didn't want us communicating with the base station back at McMurdo Sound.

I put my flashlight away, pulled out my Luger, fumbling the safety catch off with my gloved hands, and then continued forward as best I could.

Tibert's body lay crumpled in a heap beneath a section of the radio tower, his face badly mangled, and frozen blood everywhere on the snow.

He had evidently gone up the tower, and while up there someone had cut the guy wires, causing him to fall to his death.

I cursed my own stupidity for not checking to see if the others were in their rooms before I came out here. This could have happened an hour ago—giving whoever had done it time to get back to their room before I came out.

The section of tower pinning Tibert's body was dug into the snow, and too heavy for me to lift. His body would have to stay out here until the storm passed and I could get some help to remove the tower.

I started to edge back along the tower toward the generator building when an engine started somewhere out ahead of me, and I stopped. A moment later another engine started. Then two sets of headlights came on.

Snowcats. Someone was out there aboard snowtrack vehicles. The engines were revving up as I raised my Luger and fired two shots in quick succession at a point above one set of headlights. The machine seemed to lurch toward me, and then its engine died, but the headlights remained on.

The second machine was lumbering toward me as I brought my Luger around and fired two more shots.

A shot whined off the tower metal six inches away from me, and I twisted to the right as something very hot stitched across my side, knocking me off balance.

By the time I scrambled upright again, both machines had turned away and were racing into the storm, the sounds of their engines fading rapidly in the howling wind. I fired four more shots in the direction I thought they were going, and then lowered my weapon.

It hadn't been Stalnov after all, but from what Tibert had told me, I suspected it was some of Stalnov's people from their main base. The movement the lead helicopter pilot had seen below him, on the way out here yesterday, had probably been these people.

I put my Luger in my pocket and stiffly worked my way back to the base of the tower, then back around the generator building to where the guide line was attached.

Shaking with the intense cold, my entire left side aching from where the bullet had just grazed my ribs, I grabbed the rope and headed back toward the Administration building.

If anything, the wind had risen in intensity during the time I had been out here, and combined with my wound, the going was very rough.

Twice I stumbled and fell, but the second time I got to my feet the rope came loose in my hand. For a long moment I stood there holding the slack rope until I looked back the way I had come and pulled on the rope. It came taut. It was still connected to the generator building.

Turning back, I carefully pulled on the rope, and it was loose. It had either broken free from the Administration building end, or someone had cut it.

The cold was making it almost impossible to think straight, and for several seconds longer I stood there, stupidly holding the slack rope in my hands.

But then I started forward, keeping the rope taut behind me. Unless the rope had been cut very far from the Administration building, I could still follow it to the end, and then walk in an arc until I bumped into the doorway.

In ten minutes I had come to the end of the rope where it had obviously been cut, and I drew it up tight behind me so that I was at its extreme limit. I tried to peer through the darkness for a light in one of the windows. But there was nothing.

The path had been completely covered over by the snow, which was nearly hip deep by now, and I began to realize that I was completely lost.

If I let go of the rope and stumbled forward there was a very good chance I'd miss the Administration building. And in this weather I would not last very long out here.

I turned and looked back the way I had come. I was going to have to follow the rope back to the generator building. At least there was shelter from the storm and bitter cold back there. It wouldn't be very comfortable, but I wouldn't freeze to death.

I took two steps back when the rope suddenly went slack in my hand, and I stopped. Whoever it was on the snowtracks had evidently come back and cut the rope from the generator building end. They were still out there—probably with some kind of camp set up just out of sight.

Unless I could get back inside and warn the others, they would be sitting ducks. Whoever was out there could come at their leisure and pick everyone off, one by one.

I turned again in the direction I thought the Administration building lay, dropped the rope, and stumbled forward, a step at a time, stopping often as I tried to catch a glimpse of a light. But I could see nothing except the swirling snow in front of my face.

How long I wandered around out there, I'll never know, but at one point I thought I saw a light. Faint. To my left. And I turned that way.

I stumbled a few steps forward, but I could no longer see the light, and I began to wonder if I had really seen it in the first place.

But then it was there again, a soft, rosy glow, and I hurried forward through the snow as best I could.

It was a light. It was coming from a small window, and within a couple of minutes I had made it to the building, which disappeared into the impenetrable darkness to the left and right.

It was all I could do to reach the window. I was exhausted, and I didn't think I would be able to last much longer out here.

I reached up and tapped on the heavily frosted window, and immediately I could make out the figure of someone on the other side.

I tapped on the window again, and then watched as someone scraped a small hole in the frost, and looked out at me. For a moment our eyes met, and then the window slid away as my legs gave out and I sat down in the snow.

The thought crossed my mind that if it had been Stalnov looking out at me, he would not come out here to help me. He would probably lock the doors in this wing of the building, and I would never make it.

Minutes that seemed like hours later, someone was helping me to my feet. I looked up into the face of Dr. de Hoorn.

"You're too heavy," she shouted over the wind. "You must help."

I nodded, and somehow managed to stand. With my arm around her shoulder, we stumbled away from the window, down the length of the building, and then inside the building.

Just inside the door we stopped a moment to catch our breath, and then de Hoorn helped me down the corridor and into her room, where she sat me down on the edge of the bed.

She took off her parka, tossed it aside, and then unzipped mine and pulled it off.

"What were you doing out there . . ." she started to say, but then she saw the blood at my side. "Jesus," she swore, and went across the room and got her medical kit.

Back at the bed, she unbuttoned my shirt and helped me pull it off, then with a pair of scissors cut my thermal underwear top off and tossed it aside.

"You've been shot," she said examining my wound.

I looked down at my side. There was a blue cast to my skin because of the cold, except around a long, angry red slash where the bullet had grazed the ribs.

"Will I live?" I asked thickly. It was hard to talk.

"Who did this?" she snapped. She had taken out a large bottle of disinfectant from her medical kit, and she soaked some cotton battens with it. "This will sting," she said.

I gritted my teeth as she swabbed out the wound, the pain causing my stomach to turn over and the room to spin.

When she was done with that, she daubbed on some first-aid cream and then tightly bandaged my side.

"You were lucky," she said when she was finished. "None of your ribs is broken, although one of them may be cracked." I looked up at her as she put a stethoscope to her ears and placed the pickup over my heart.

The lights seemed to be getting dimmer, and I was cold now, even colder than I had been when I was outside.

"Hypothermia," she said half to herself, laying the stethoscope aside. She grabbed my arms and pulled me to my feet, and then balancing me there with one hand, pulled the covers back on the bed and sat me back down.

Gently, she pushed me on my back, removed my boots and socks, and then pulled off my trousers and thermal underwear.

I felt like a small child being undressed by his mother, and yet I was so cold and numb, I could do nothing but passively go along with her.

She began peeling off her clothes then, and in a few seconds she was nude, the nipples on her large breasts erect. She was a good-looking woman, her body firm and well proportioned.

"During the Second World War, the Nazi doctors did teach us how to deal with hypothermia," she said as she crawled into bed with me and flipped the covers up over us.

Carefully she snuggled up against me, her legs intertwining with mine. Her skin seemed hot, almost on fire as she rubbed her hands down my back, and moved her body alongside mine.

Almost immediately I had an overwhelming urge to make love to her, but I tried to pull away.

"No," she said softly. "It's all right. It's natural. It will warm you."

She rolled over on her back, pulling me on top of her as she spread her legs, and then she guided me inside of her, and slowly we made love, my pulse throbbing in my ears, a wonderfully warm flush spreading throughout my body from my loins.

"This is good, Nicholas," she whispered in my ear. "This is very good," she said, breathing heavily.

When we were done, I did not have the strength to roll over, and she had to help me. But I was warm now.

She slipped out of the bed, and covered me up again. "You will sleep now," she said.

I looked up at her, everything dim in my eyes. "Tibert is dead," I mumbled, but I didn't think she heard me.

"It's all right, Nicholas," she said. "Sleep now. I will make excuses to the others for your absence. But you must sleep."

I tried to raise up, but I couldn't, and the room went gradually dark as I drifted off to a warm, dreamless sleep.

I awoke to the sound of the howling wind, and for a brief, disorienting few seconds I thought I was still outside, the slack guide rope in my hands.

But then what happened and where I was came back to me in a rush, and I sat up with a start; a sharp pain stabbed at me from my side.

My watch read a few minutes after noon, and although I was chilly again and my side hurt, I felt a hell of a lot better than I had last night when Elsie de Hoorn had helped me.

I shoved the covers back and was just getting out of

bed when the door opened and she came in, a concerned expression on her face.

She closed the door, came across the room to me, checked my pulse, and then my temperature.

"You seem a lot better," she said, tersely. "How do you feel?"

"Alive," I said looking up at her. "Did we make love last night, or was I dreaming?"

A faint flicker of a smile crossed her face, and then was gone. "Commander Tibert is missing," she said. "Everyone is clamoring for a search party to go out and find you both."

"Did you tell them I was here?"

"Obviously not," she snapped. "Now what the hell happened last night? Who shot you, and where is Commander Tibert?"

"How about going down to my room and getting me some fresh clothes while I clean up. I'll explain it all to you then."

She nodded, turned on her heel, and left the room as I got up and washed up as best I could at the sink in the corner.

A couple of minutes later she was back with my clothes, and I quickly got dressed, strapping on my weapons as she watched.

When I was finished, I lit myself a cigarette and inhaled deeply.

"A very bad habit," she said automatically.

"Commander Tibert is dead," I said without preamble, and Elsie sucked in her breath.

"My God," she said. "What is happening here?"

For just a moment I debated telling her anything, but then I decided that she would have to be warned.

"There was some trouble with the communications radio last night. Tibert went out to check the tower.

When he was up top, the tower collapsed and he fell to his death.''

"An accident?" she asked.

I shook my head. "He was lured out there, and when he was up on the tower, someone cut the guy wires, causing it to collapse."

"Who shot you?"

"I don't know for sure," I said. And quickly I explained what had happened last night.

She absorbed all this in grim-lipped silence, and when I was finished her complexion was somewhat white. "Have you got another cigarette?"

I lit one for her, and she puffed on it with shaking hands. "It still does not answer who killed him, and why. Do you think it was the Russians?"

"Possibly," I said. "Stalnov is no scientist. He's probably KGB."

She nodded. "Why would they want you and Commander Tibert dead?"

"They might want us all dead, Elsie," I said softly.

Her hand holding the cigarette shook so badly she almost dropped it. "Why? In heaven's name, why?"

I told her then about the secret laboratory beneath the generator building, and what Tibert had explained to me about the Russians' work on the Rapid Varying Bio-Agent materials.

"That still doesn't explain what killed these people. If Commander Tibert was telling the truth, and the prime materials were tagged, we would have found residuals in the bodies. That is not the case."

"I know," I said. "Which means someone killed these people to stop their research, or there was an accident."

"Antidotes do not kill people."

"I know that too," I said. "I think it was the Soviet RVB-A that killed them. It was either introduced to this area on purpose, or by accident."

"By the Russians?"

"By the Russians," I said.

Elsie looked away for a moment. "Then Stalnov's job on this commission would be to cover up the accident or the murder."

"Exactly," I said.

"But why kill Commander Tibert?" she asked. "That doesn't make sense. It only serves to prove your theory."

"I instructed Commander Tibert to radio our base installation at McMurdo Sound, and order up an air surveillance of the coast." I explained to her why I thought it was possible that the Soviets would be transporting the RVB-A to a submarine rendezvous.

She thought about that for a moment. "Except for the fact that you have suffered a gunshot wound, I would guess that what you have told me is nothing more than a paranoid delusion. But under the circumstances, there may be something in what you've said."

"Thank you for that," I replied.

"What do you want me to do, Nicholas?" she asked. "I will help, if I can."

"Say nothing," I said. "You have not seen me since yesterday evening in the dining hall. No matter what is said or done, you have not seen me. Agreed?"

"Agreed," she said after a moment of uncertainty.

CHAPTER SEVEN

Although it was daytime now, it was almost impossible to see anything through the blowing snow. The storm had increased in fury during the night, and as I crawled on my hands and knees around the huge, fantastically-shaped snowdrifts, from the east wing around to the front of the Administration building, I couldn't help but wonder how Tibert's murderers were faring out in their encampment.

If this kept up, there was a good chance, I thought, that they would not survive.

It took me nearly an hour to make it less than fifty yards around the building to the front entrance where I had to dig my way down through a huge snowdrift to get at the door.

If I was going to catch Stalnov off guard, Elsie de Hoorn was going to have to play her role with an absolutely straight face. The Russian had already proved his abilities as an investigator. And he would certainly notice Elsie's reaction if she was a bad actress.

The door was frozen shut and it took me several minutes to break it free, then swing it open and step down into the antarctic vestibule. When I had the outer door closed, I opened the inner door and stepped inside.

Everyone was in the dayroom. Kurt Abel, the West German, was holding a .45 automatic with a shaking hand; when I flipped my hood back, and they all saw it was me. He lowered the weapon.

"Mein Gott," he said softly.

"Nicholas!" Lana cried out, and she started toward me, then stopped.

"Where were you?" Abel said. "We searched everywhere this morning."

"I spent the night in the generator building," I said. I kept my eyes on Stalnov, who didn't blink.

"Why?" Lana asked. "What happened?"

"Let's go into the dining hall. I could use some hot coffee, and something to eat," I said.

We all went through the day room and into the dining hall, where Lana and Elsie brought me coffee and some bacon and eggs that they had made earlier.

Everyone sat around the long table and watched me eat, Lana and Abel the most agitated of them. If Stalnov knew what had happened out there last night, he wasn't showing it this morning.

When I was finished I lit myself a cigarette. They were all waiting for my explanation.

"Commander Tibert is dead," I said.

Stalnov seemed as shocked as the others. He sat forward. "I think you had better explain what is happening here, Captain Carter," he said.

"He tried to send a status report to our base camp last night, but there was something apparently wrong with the antenna," I said. "He went out to check on it, and when he didn't return, I went out after him."

"What happened to him?" Lana asked. There was a fearful expression on her face.

"It was an accident," I said. "He climbed up the tower, a gust of wind or something snapped the guy wires, the tower collapsed, and he fell to his death."

"My God," Elsie de Hoorn said, bringing one hand to her mouth. She was doing a superb job of acting.

"But why didn't you come back immediately?" Lana asked.

"The storm was too bad out there, and I was afraid of getting lost."

"Surely there is a guide rope between the two buildings," Stalnov said.

"I couldn't find it," I said. "It's probably buried in the snow."

"We're going to have to radio for help," Lana said.

"The radio tower is down, Dr. Edwards," Stalnov said.

"I'm going to dig out one of the helicopters this morning and use its radio," I said. "But I'm not going to call for help. We don't need any. We're here to do a job, and we're going to finish it."

Lana started to argue with me, but I cut her off.

"Dr. de Hoorn, have you and the others come up with anything positive from the autopsies?"

"Not yet," she said.

Dr. Straub, who had been helping on the pathology team, took his pipe out of his mouth. "I set up a dozen cultures from tissue samples last night. I should have some results within a few hours," he said.

"Then we'll know what killed these people?" I asked. For the first time there was a look of worry on Stalnov's face, but Straub was shaking his head.

"I didn't say that, Captain. I said we'll have some results. Nothing more. A beginning."

"I see," I said after a moment. Then I looked up. "In the meantime, I don't want anyone to go outside for any reason. The storm is very bad. I wouldn't want another accident."

"We're finished with this wing of the complex, in any event," Abel said. "We'll begin on the laboratories then. Unless you would like some help outside digging out one of the helicopters."

"I'll manage, Doctor," I said. "Your time will be better spent in the laboratory." I stood up. "I want to know what killed these people, and where it came from."

Stalnov was getting to his feet. "What do you mean by that?"

"Whatever killed these people didn't come from this installation."

"What are you saying, Nicholas?" Lana asked.

"Nothing was going on here that could have killed our people," I said.

"We can't be sure of that until our tests are finished," Straub snapped. He too got to his feet and went to the door where he stopped and turned back. "One thing is for sure," he said. "Sitting here sipping coffee and speculating will get us absolutely no where."

No one said a thing, and Straub continued:

"I admire your loyalty to your government, Captain Carter, but this is an *international* commission. And our job is to find out what killed these people, so that we can prevent it from happening elsewhere. And I for one intend to do my job."

He left the room, and a moment later everyone else, except for Lana, got up and left as well.

When we were alone, she poured me another cup of coffee and then sat back down across the table from me, a firm expression on her face.

"What really happened out there last night?" she asked, in low tones.

Besides Elsie de Hoorn, Lana was the only other person I could trust here. And as much as I didn't want to do it, I felt I had to warn her.

"Tibert was murdered," I said.

Lana's complexion turned white. "How?"

I told her what had happened, including the fact that someone had shot at me and then cut the guide rope at both ends.

"Then you must radio for help," she said.

"I will," I said. "But in the meantime I want you to find a weapon, in case whoever out there tries for one of us."

"Who else knows about this?"

"Dr. de Hoorn," I said.

"It's the Russians, isn't it? Stalnov is here to cover up."

I nodded, then reached out for her hand. "You've got to keep yourself together, Lana. If Stalnov suspects that you know something, he won't hesitate to kill you."

"I don't know . . ." she said, letting it trail off.

"You've got to help me. Just a little longer."

"Why don't you just arrest him?"

I shook my head. "We'd never find out what really happened here. And besides, his buddies are out there someplace." I quickly explained what Tibert had told me about the Soviets' work with RVB-A substances, and our work on a universal antidote.

"Then it's true," she said, looking away momentarily. "There's been some discussion about the possibility, but I didn't think it had come this far."

"Apparently it has."

"But why, Nick? Why would the Russians kill these people. They must have realized that there would have been an investigation."

"I don't think they did it on purpose," I said. "I think they may have been transporting the material to a rendezvous with a submarine. There may have been an accident."

"They'd be looking for it then," she said.

"That's right. And Stalnov was sent here to make sure that we don't come up with that answer."

"He'd kill us if he knew."

"Exactly."

She thought about that for several long seconds, the full realization of just how precarious our position here was slowly coming to her. When she finally looked up, there was a new, determined expression on her face. "What do you want me to do?"

"Find a weapon, then go about your business as if you don't know a thing. I'll get one of the helicopters dug out and get a message off to McMurdo Sound this morning. If there is a sub out there, we can't let them find the substance and get it aboard. If they somehow get it back to Moscow it would be a powerful weapon that we have no defense for. At least not yet."

"There would be war."

"Almost immediately," I said.

We got up and I went to the door with her.

"I'm frightened, Nick," she said.

"Just keep out of Stalnov's way," I said. I kissed her. "Everything is going to turn out all right."

She smiled up at me, nodded, and then went down the corridor. We were in an almost impossible position here, with Stalnov on the inside, and his people on the outside. But telling her that would not have accomplished much of anything.

I hurried through the day room and down the west wing to where the things from the supply room that we were using as a pathology laboratory had been piled.

After ten minutes of hunting through the jumbled mess, I managed to find a shovel and a coil of rope, which I took back to the main outside door off the day room.

Before I went back outside, I snapped a fresh clip in my Luger and placed the gun in my parka pocket. Then I bundled up, grabbed the rope and the shovel, and pushed my way outside, into the raging storm.

The wind was very strong now, making it totally impossible to stand, or do much more than huddle in the snow. Laying the shovel down, I managed to tie one end of the rope around the big door handle. The other end I tied around my waist.

Making sure there were no snarls in the coil of rope, I grabbed the shovel, and crawled out away from the building in the direction I thought the two helicopters lay. They would be mostly buried beneath the snow, but I was hoping that one of the rotors might be jutting out, or that I could at least recognize a hump in the snow where they were covered.

Nearly an hour later I came to the end of the rope without finding anything. I was at least sixty or seventy yards away from the building and reasonably certain I was as far out as the helicopters. I had missed them.

Keeping the rope taut, I started crawling to the left, the going almost impossible through the drifts.

I stopped at one point to listen; I thought I had heard the low-pitched whine of a snowcat engine. But I didn't hear it again, and ten minutes later I wasn't sure if I had heard anything other than the wind.

The cold was penetrating, and I could feel a wetness at my side where my wound had evidently opened and I was bleeding.

I would not be able to stay out here much longer. If I stopped too long to rest I would almost certainly freeze to death.

The rope snagged on something between me and the Administration building, and I had to stop to try and free it. But after a couple of minutes of trying, the rope still would not come free, and I began crawling back along its length.

Ten minutes later I stumbled across something hard, and I turned back to look. A part of a helicopter rotor was exposed. My rope had gotten caught beneath the tip.

I freed the rope, then using the shovel, uncovered the rotor back to its hub, where I started digging down.

Within a few minutes I was hot and sweating, but I had dug deep enough down into the snow along the side of the helicopter so that I was fairly well protected from the wind, although snow kept drifting down into my hole, filling it in.

Finally, I managed to dig down to the side cargo door of the machine where I hit the latch, and the door swung heavily inward, a lot of snow avalanching into the machine.

I crawled inside, completely out of the wind now, untied the rope around my waist, and made it forward to the pilot's seat.

For a long time I sat there trying to catch my breath, my lungs aching from the intense cold, my heart hammering in my chest, and the wound throbbing at my side.

After a while I sat forward, studied the control panel for a moment, then flipped on the main switch. The battery indicator came up well over half charge, and I switched on the radio, the interior of the helicopter immediately filling with the hiss and pop of a communications receiver.

I found the microphone, picked it up, and was about to hit the push-to-talk switch, when I smelled aviation fuel.

Except for the lights on the control panel, the interior of the helicopter was dark. I laid the mike down, pulled out my penlight from an inside pocket, switched it on, and shined it back toward the cargo area.

At first I couldn't see a thing, but then I noticed a wet patch on the deck. Something was dripping on the deck from above.

I crawled out of the pilot's seat and worked my way back to the cargo bay where the smell of aviation fuel was very strong.

There was a high-pitched buzzing coming from above, and I directed the tiny beam of light that way. The helicopter's fuel pump was on and leaking badly, spraying aviation gas all over the interior of the cargo bay.

For a long second I stared up at the spray. Something had gone wrong with the machine. Evidently, the main switch had shorted alongside the fuel pump switch, and at the same time there was a leak in the system.

Naturally, the chances of that happening had to be astronomical.

I looked back at the instrument panel. The gyros were running, the lights were on. A spark. Any kind of a spark, once the helicopter filled with aviation gas fumes, would cause an explosion.

Suddenly I realized that someone else had gotten to the helicopter before me.

I pocketed my flashlight, grabbed the rope, and scrambled out of the machine and up the steep snowbank, and rolled over the edge into the storm.

It wouldn't take very long for the gas fumes to build up to an explosive mixture. That was my only thought as I followed the rope, hand over hand, back toward the Administration building as fast as I could crawl.

I don't think I had made it more than twenty or twenty-five yards, when a tremendous force lifted me completely off my hands and knees, and threw me forward at least ten feet.

The dull, deep-throated thump came almost simultaneously, followed by a blast of hot air and rain from the instantly melted snow.

My parka was on fire from the fuel that had sprayed on me in the cargo bay, but I was able to easily put out the flames by rolling around in the snow.

Bits of the helicopter were scattered around me; except for a scorched parka I was unhurt.

As I got to my hands and knees once again, the wind-whipped flames from the explosion were already starting to die down.

There was little doubt that the other machine, buried in the snow, had been booby-trapped as well. Had I not smelled the gas fumes when I had, I would have died in the explosion.

But now I had a decision to make. In this storm no one could possibly know if I had survived the explosion or not. If I remained under cover somewhere within the installation, Stalnov and his troops would think that I was dead. If I returned to the others, Stalnov would have to know that I was aware someone was trying to stop the commission.

There were advantages and disadvantages to both courses of action.

If I didn't show myself, Stalnov would feel that he had a free hand, and he would be more likely to make a crucial, incriminating mistake. But, if I didn't show up, there would be no restraints on him. It wasn't inconceivable that he would murder the others.

If I did return to the Administration building, Stalnov would be on his guard, but he would not try anything against the others. Not until I was dead.

I scrambled around until I found the rope. But then I stopped a moment. There was an alternative. A risky one, admittedly, but one that would take most of the danger away from the others . . . and perhaps force

Stalnov's people to make a decisive move.

I tried to think out all the ramifications, but it was like a chess game—any one good move could bring about any number of countermoves. The only way to find out for sure what the enemy was going to do was to make a move and wait for the countermove.

As the flames behind me died to nothing, I worked my way back along the rope to the administration building. It had taken fifteen minutes to get to the door, where I stumbled into the day room.

Stalnov was there, and as I tumbled into the room I reached for my Luger as he hurried forward. But he helped me to my feet.

"I saw the explosion! What happened out there?" he asked.

Straub and Abel came from the corridor on the run.

"What happened?"

"Are you all right?" they shouted.

Stalnov was either an excellent actor (which I suspected was the case) or he was innocent of any knowledge of the booby-trapped helicopter.

"There was a leak in the helicopter's fuel system. I had just gotten out when it exploded," I said.

"Did you get a message off?" Stalnov asked.

I looked directly in his eyes. "No. But I've decided to go for help."

"How?" he asked.

"I'm sure there are snowtrack vehicles here. I'm going to take one and drive it back to McMurdo."

"Impossible in this weather," Abel said.

"No," Stalnov interjected. "It could be done. We could rig some kind of a homing device, on McMurdo's base radio station."

"That's what I thought," I said.

Someone shouted something in the west corridor, and

a moment later Lana burst into the dayroom.

"Nick!" she screamed. "It's Elsie . . . she's . . . dead!"

Straub had spun around. "What?" he shouted.

"She's dead! It's horrible!" Lana screeched nearly incoherently.

Straub reached her first and slapped her across the face. Instantly she stopped screaming. A second later I was at her side.

"What is it, Lana?" I asked.

She looked up at me. "She's dead. Elsie . . . Dr. de Hoorn is dead."

"Where?"

"In the lab."

"Show me," I said.

"No," Straub shouted. I looked at him. "We discussed this, Captain Carter. We knew that there could be an accident with the bodies."

"What are you saying?" I snapped.

"My cultures came back positive," he said. "The people here were killed by an airborne culture that they breathed. But most importantly, the culture was absorbed into their tissues."

"What are you saying to me?"

"The bodies are all deadly. They're still carrying the agent that killed them."

Stalnov seemed as surprised as the others.

"You can come with me," Straub said. "But we must dress in our biological safe suits."

I looked at Lana. "Did you touch anything in there?"

She shook her head. "I went in to talk to her. But she was lying on the floor in front of the table. She was . . . dead . . . like the others."

I nodded at Straub and went across the day room to where we had left our bio suits when we had first gotten here. We were dressed in a couple of minutes, the helmets sealed, and the compressed air flowing.

Straub motioned for the others to remain in the day room, and the two of us went back down the west corridor and into the pathology lab that had been set up in the supply room.

A male cadaver was lying on a table in the middle of the room. On the floor, beside it, Elsie de Hoorn lay on her back, her eyes open, her tongue protruding from her mouth and the blood down her chin. She looked like she had been in great pain just before she died.

Quickly Dr. Straub went to her and did a quick examination. When he stood up, I could see his concern, even through the face plate of his helmet.

"Her spine is broken, her muscles are ripped," his voice came over my suit radio.

"The same agent that killed the others?"

Straub looked down at Elsie, and then at the cadaver. "The same," he said. "The agent is still active."

CHAPTER EIGHT

It was already starting to get dark when Stalnov came back out to the maintenance garage with the maps. We had worked most of the afternoon together getting one of the installation's snowcats ready for the one hundred and fifty mile trip back to McMurdo Bay. Between us we had managed to jury rig a crude radio direction finder from some of the equipment in the radio room.

"Your track won't be perfectly straight," Stalnov had cautioned. "But the closer you come to the base, the more accurate your readings will be."

The machine was fully fueled, there were emergency rations on board, and an arctic shelter tent and catalytic heater.

Outside, the wind was howling in its full fury, and as Stalnov came across the garage to me, he looked toward the service doors and shook his head.

"It doesn't sound too good out there," I said.

He shook his head again. "I don't understand why you feel you must return to your base at this moment. Why don't you wait for the storm to abate?"

"We've gone over that before," I said. "I want to get back to let them know everything is all right out here. After what happened in the first place, everyone—including your own government—will be very nervous. As soon as the storm lifts I'll be back with a helicopter and new radio gear."

Stalnov looked at me for a long moment, probably wondering how much of what I was telling him was the truth, and how much else I knew or had guessed.

"Then you will have to be very careful, Captain Carter," he said. He spread the map open on the back cargo shelf of my snowcat and quickly pointed out four broad areas between us and McMurdo Sound where there was a high frequency of crevasses.

"There is a crevasse detector aboard your machine," he said. "Works like sonar, but the equipment is basically the same as what we use. Not a hundred percent reliable."

He looked up at me. "In these areas you will have to go very slow. Allow for the detector to make several sweeps."

I studied the map for several seconds. The first area of crevasses was around ten miles out on a direct heading back to McMurdo. I figured that Stalnov's troops were probably camped somewhere between here and there. If I could get past the first area of crevasses, the remainder of the trip would be relatively trouble free.

At last I folded the map and put it inside the snow-track. "Thanks for your help," I said.

Stalnov shook my hand. "I wish you much luck, Captain," he said.

"I'll make it," I said. "I don't have any doubts about it. But while I'm gone I want you to keep a close eye on everyone. I wouldn't want any more accidents to happen."

"I understand," Stalnov said. From inside his parka, he produced a bottle of brandy. "In this weather the trip will take you at least ten hours. Perhaps during one of your rest stops you might care to have a drink."

I took the bottle from him. The seal was still intact, so I didn't think he had tampered with the liquor. More likely the gesture was nothing more than the last drink for a condemned man.

"Thanks," I said. I put the bottle behind the front seat, then climbed in behind the controls.

"Goodbye Captain," Stalnov said.

"See you later," I replied, and I slammed the door and started the engine as Stalnov put the hood of his parka up, then went to the service door and swung it open.

I put the snowtrack in gear, and the machine lumbered forward, up the steep snowbank, and I was outside, my headlights not penetrating the snow and darkness much more than ten or fifteen feet.

I swung around the main building, then headed past the generator building and the downed antenna, directly away from the installation. About a half mile out, I stopped in the blinding snowstorm and turned the direction finder to McMurdo's weather service radio station. At this distance the signal was unclear, and was breaking up badly, but it was enough for me to take an approximate bearing from the RDF.

With the map spread out on my lap I drew the radio bearing to the American installation on the sound, then drew another line farther to the right, to the Soviet installation which was fifty miles farther up the coast.

The difference in bearings at this distance only amounted to a degree or two, so as long as I kept slightly to the right of the RDF track, I would make it to the Soviet installation.

I set the map aside, turned off the dome light, and headed into the storm, the crevasse scanner searching for cracks in the ice out ahead of me, my headlights doing little more than keeping me company, and the drone of the engine the only other noise besides the howling, raging wind.

As I drove I thought about poor Elsie de Hoorn, the thirtieth innocent victim in this little war. Paul Tibert had at least suspected what he was going up against, and he had had the ability to defend himself—unlike the others. He had simply made a mistake, the most costly mistake of all.

I was making between fifteen and twenty miles an hour over the uneven ice and snow; about half an hour out I stopped again.

I was coming close to the first area of crevasses that Stalnov had marked on my map, so I was going to have to be careful now over the next few miles.

The McMurdo weather signal still wasn't any stronger, but my second bearing showed that I was fairly close on track.

I studied the map for a few moments. The main lines of crevasses seemed to run at right angles to my path, so that if I wanted to cross the area safely I was going to have to turn east for a couple of miles, then cut back to the northwest.

The snowcat's engine was idling, and I held the clutch down with my left foot as I put the map aside. Just as I was about ready to take off, a figure appeared at the windshield and I looked up.

It was a man, dressed in white cold weather gear. He was pointing a Kalashnikov assault rifle at me.

Slowly I took my hands off the steering column and raised them above my head.

The man at the windshield nodded, and a second later the door on my side started to come open. At that moment I ducked low to the left as I pressed down on the accelerator pedal and popped the clutch.

The snowcat lurched forward at the same moment a

single shot was fired through the windshield, and I could feel the left track passing over the man with the rifle.

I yanked my Luger out, then locked the snowcat's left track so that it would continue circling that way. Next I crawled over to the passenger side, careful to keep beneath the level of the windshield, unlatched the door, then shoved it open and tumbled outside into the storm.

A half dozen shots were fired at the snowtrack from the left. An instant later I was up on my knee, and I fired four shots in rapid succession that way.

Someone cried out over the noise of the storm, and as I dove behind the circling machine several more shots were fired toward where I had just been.

I stumbled to my feet and pushed my way through the snow—keeping beside the slowly moving snowcat.

For a minute or two, there were no sounds except the snowcat's lumbering engine and the wind. Then I began to hear another sound.

A shot whined off the roof of my machine, and I ducked a little lower, straining to listen for the other sound.

Then I had it. I could hear another snowtrack vehicle idling out there somewhere. It couldn't be too far away or I would not be able to hear it over the wind.

The last shots had been fired far to my right, and I turned and snapped off two quick shots, then hurried around the front of my machine, keeping just ahead of it until I got to the other side where I ducked down low in the snow.

My snowtrack lumbered off into the storm and out of sight as a couple of more shots were fired at it from my right.

Then I could hear the sound of the idling snowtrack vehicle just behind me, and I turned and crawled toward it.

Within about twenty feet I came to the large machine,

its headlights off, its engine slowly turning over.

I crawled around to the rear window and cautiously stood up so that I could look inside. A cold-weather-suited figure was seated behind the steering column, and as I watched, he picked up a microphone and said something I couldn't quite catch.

The reply over his radio was clear though.

"He's behind his machine," the radio crackled.

"Destroy it," the man behind the steering column said.

I ducked down below the level of the rear window, crawled back to the passenger side door, and then listened again.

"Hurry," the man inside said.

The radio crackled. "We're getting around behind it . . ."

I jerked open the door and raised my Luger so that it was pointing directly at the Russian's head, just a few inches away from his temple.

"Key the microphone and you are a dead man, comrade," I said in Russian.

The man's eyes widened as he looked at me and then my gun from the corner of his eyes. He held the microphone in his right hand, and I could see that he wanted to press the push-to-talk switch.

"I will put a bullet through your brain. I promise you," I said. "Is it worth it?"

"His machine is circling," the radio blared.

"Get behind it. On the other side," another voice came from the speaker.

"Put the microphone down, comrade. Now!"

The driver did as I said, and I carefully climbed up into the machine and slammed the door behind me.

"What do you want?" the Russian asked.

"How many people are out there?"

"Three," he said after a slight hesitation.

"How many at your camp?"

"None," he said.

"You are lying. Before I killed Comrade Stalnov, he told me there were at least ten of you."

"I just talked with . . ." the driver blurted, but then he realized his mistake, and he cut himself off.

I smiled and brought the barrel of the Luger a little closer to the man's head. "Cooperate now, or I will kill you. How many at your camp?"

"One other team of four," the Russian said. "One of them is seriously wounded."

"Where is the camp?"

"You passed it on your way out."

"I've found Dmitri," the radio blared. The driver started to reach for the microphone, but I shook my head.

"Peter . . . Peter . . . I have found Dmitri. He is dead."

Several shots were fired out in the storm, and a moment later the radio blared: "I have stopped his machine."

"The bastard," the other man radioed. "We should leave him out here to freeze to death."

"Let's go," I said.

The driver looked at me, his eyes wide. "Where?"

"McMurdo Sound," I said.

"But . . . we cannot leave them out here. They will die."

"No they won't," I said. "There are emergency rations, a tent, and a heater aboard my machine. They'll live until the storm is over. Now move it, comrade!"

The Russian hesitated. I reached up and snapped the ejector slide back on my Luger, the noise loud inside the machine. "Move it or die!"

The Russian put the snowtrack in gear and slowly

lumbered out into the storm.

"Peter?" the radio blared.

"Faster," I snapped.

"Vasily . . . it is Peter . . . he is leaving."

"Peter?" the man screamed. "Peter?"

I reached out and clicked the radio off, then sat back and with one hand pulled a cigarette from my inner pocket and lit it. "McMurdo Sound," I said. "But I want you to be very careful of the crevasses. It wouldn't do for us to have an accident."

"My radio direction finder is set for my own base, and it is crystal controlled so I cannot retune it for your antenna on the American installation."

"That's fine," I said. "I want to go to your base."

The Russian looked sharply at me, and I smiled again.

"There are a couple of questions I'd like to ask your people there," I said.

Without warning I ripped the microphone, cord and all, from the communications radio, opened the window flap, and tossed it outside. Now, no matter what happened, there would be no communications to Stalnov, or to the base at McMurdo Sound. We were alone out here, just the two of us, and would remain alone until we finally came to the coast, more than a hundred and twenty-five miles away.

The crevasse detector pinged a moment later, and almost nonchalantly the driver eased his machine to the left for a hundred yards or so, then sharply to the right, coming back on track a minute or two later.

He did the same thing at least a half dozen times, until we were past the area of crevasses. Obviously the path had been mapped out for him through the crevasses.

"What were your people doing camped out near our installation?" I asked.

The driver glanced at me but said nothing. He was a

relatively young man, and I felt somewhat sorry for him.
He was caught now in a very difficult position, between
his orders and my Luger. But a lot of good people were
dead because of what the Soviets were doing down here.
I didn't want the number to grow.

"You know, Peter, I am a man of very small patience.
You can either answer my questions, or I will kill you.
I'm sure I can find my way back to the Sound with this
machine."

Again the young man glanced at me, a fearful look in
his eyes. "What do you want?" he asked finally.

"What were your people doing out there?"

"We were sent to make sure none of you left the base,
or communicated with your own people."

"Why?"

"I don't know," he said shaking his head.

"Not good enough," I snapped.

"I swear it. I do not know."

"How long were you supposed to stay out there?"

"Until we were told our job was finished."

"Who was supposed to tell you that, and how?"

"Comrade Stalnov, by radio."

Stalnov, by radio. I sat back in my seat. Most likely
Stalnov had watched Tibert leave the radio room and go
outside to fix whatever was wrong with the tower—a
malfunction that his troops had engineered earlier. Once
he was sure that Tibert was up the tower, he had ordered
his people to cut the guy wires. So simple.

"Who cut the guy wires on our radio tower?" I asked.

The young man looked at me, real fear in his eyes
now. "You?" I asked.

He shook his head. "No . . . it was . . . I do not know.
We were ordered. We are soldiers."

"How about the others out there? Will Stalnov order
their deaths as well?"

"No," he said. "Not unless they try to escape."

"Like me?"

The young Russian said nothing, and I didn't press him any further. He was a soldier, doing nothing more than his job.

The storm began to die off slightly around two in the morning when we were still an hour or so away from the Soviet installation on McMurdo Sound.

The radio direction finding signals were very loud and steady now, and we were well past the final area of crevasses.

What I was about to do next was very dangerous, but I knew of no other way of making sure what was going on down here than to go to the source. It would be very early in the morning when we got there, a time when the night-shift people would be the least alert. We were not expected, so far as I knew. And the Soviet installation wasn't a military base as such, so I figured the security here would be fairly lax.

"Are there any guards on the gate?" I asked, finally breaking the long silence between us.

The young man looked up, startled at the sound of my voice. "What?" he asked.

"Guards. Are there any guards posted on the base?"

"No," he said.

"Any posted or off limits areas on the base?"

"The labs."

"How about the communications center?" I asked.

Again the young man seemed startled. "There are no guards. Certain . . . doors are locked . . . that's all."

"I'm going to tell you comething now, Peter, and I want you to believe it, because it will be the absolute truth. Do you understand what I am saying?"

He nodded with uncertainty.

"You are going to take me to the communications center where I want to talk with the chief operator on duty this morning."

"You cannot . . ."

"But I can, and I will, Peter. But now, this is the important part for you to understand. I will not destroy or offer any harm to the equipment there, nor will I hurt you or any of your people. I want information only."

"I cannot do this."

"Let me amend my last remark. I will not hurt you or anyone else on the base unless I am forced into it. You and your people meant to kill me. I, on the other hand, wish to hurt no one. I just want information." The Russian language seemed so formal.

"I will be considered a traitor if I help you."

"Not with a gun in your back, Peter. Even your own people are not that blind."

The young man fell silent again, and as he drove, I put my last full clip of ammunition in my Luger, then reached inside my thickly insulated trousers and removed the tiny gas bomb strapped high on my thigh in a specially designed pouch, and put it in an outer pocket.

Although the wind still blew the snow in thick sheets reducing visibility to near zero at most times, the storm was beginning to subside. It would be several hours before it cleared off, however, giving me plenty of time to do what I had to do, and then get out.

About five miles out from the Soviet base, we passed a small flag on a plastic rod stuck in the snow, and the young man turned left and sped up. Within a hundred yards we passed a second marker flag, and a hundred yards later a third.

Peter reached out and turned off the RDF. "The flags will guide us in now," he said.

"Don't be a hero," I said. "I do not wish to hurt you, but I will not hesitate if you make the slightest move to betray me."

Ten minutes later I picked out a flashing white light to the left. "What is that?" I snapped.

"The runway. It is the light on the tower."

We passed a low building next to the road on the right a couple of minutes later, and then we were inside the Soviet Antarctic Installation at McMurdo Sound, the young Russian's knuckles white where he gripped the steering column.

"No heroics, Peter," I said softly.

He looked at me.

"I will be gone within twenty minutes, and then you can sound the alarm. But until then, don't make me hurt anyone."

The installation seemed deserted at this hour of the morning, and we passed unchallenged across the base, where Peter pulled up and stopped in front of a low, expansive building bristling with antennae.

"Leave the engine running," I said. I opened my door and stepped outside into the biting cold, holding the Luger on him. "Now slide across to me. You're getting out on this side, Peter. But carefully."

The young man did as I told him, and I stepped back as he climbed out of the snowtrack and closed the door.

Together we went up the drifted-over path, and entered the building, the warmth and smell of electronic equipment unmistakable. We were in some kind of office, the lights very low, a corridor running straight back through the building.

I put my Luger in my pocket, but kept my finger on the trigger. "Where will the duty officer be at this hour?"

"In the back, I think."

"Let's go," I said.

Reluctantly Peter walked down the corridor, where at the end he stopped at a thick metal door equipped with a buzzer and a peephole about eye level.

"You've got a message from Comrade Stalnov that has to get out immediately," I whispered.

Peter pressed the buzzer as I took my Luger out and pressed the barrel against his side.

"No mistakes, Peter," I whispered.

A moment later someone was at the door. "What is it?" a voice came from a speaker in the ceiling overhead.

"I have a message which must go out," Peter said.

"In the morning."

I pressed the gun a little harder against Peter's side.

"Now," he said. "It must go out this morning. It is from Comrade Stalnov."

"All right," the voice came from the speaker, and the door lock buzzed.

CHAPTER NINE

Peter stepped through the door into the communications center, and just as I was coming through he suddenly leaped to the left.

"He has a gun!" he shouted.

I shoved him off balance, and he stumbled forward. I jumped all the way inside and slammed the thick metal door behind me.

"Sound the alarm and you all die!" I shouted, raising my Luger.

Besides the man who had opened the door for us, there were four others in the large room, which was filled with teletype and radio equipment.

One of the radio operators across the room from us was raising a microphone to his lips, and I fired a single shot just past him into the radio gear.

"Put it down," I shouted.

The man had spun around. He looked from me to the man who had opened the door, then back to me. Finally he set the microphone back down on the desk.

"Step away from there, into the center of the room," I snapped.

He did as I told him, his hands over his head.

"The rest of you, away from your positions! Now!"

The others complied as well, including Peter, who

picked himself up from the floor and fearfully stepped to the center of the room.

"Who is in charge here this morning?" I asked.

No one said a thing.

I raised the Luger and pointed it directly at the man who had let us in. He was dressed in a Soviet Navy uniform and was in his early forties, a touch of gray at his temple.

"Me," he said.

"Your name and rank?"

"Nikolai Pitrovinov, Lieutenant J.G."

"All right Lieutenant J.G. Pitrovinov, I'm going to ask you some questions, you are going to give me the answers without hesitation, and then I am going to leave. No one will get hurt if you do exactly as I say."

The man nodded.

A siren sounded from outside in the corridor, and Pitrovinov smiled.

"Nothing to smile about, Lieutenant," I said. "Now I am a very desperate man. Likely to kill someone."

The smile left his face. "You will never get out of here alive."

"There is a submarine rendezvousing off the coast somewhere. I want to know if it has arrived yet, or if it hasn't, when it will, and exactly where it will be stationed."

Someone was out in the corridor, and a second later the person was pounding at the door.

"Quickly now, Lieutenant!" I barked.

The door buzzer sounded, and someone else was pounding.

I raised the Luger with both hands, centered the sights on the lieutenant's face, and started to squeeze the trigger.

"No!" he shouted. "The submarine will be here in forty-eight hours."

"Where?" I asked. "Exactly where?"

"At the end of the Sound directly below Mt. Sabine," he said.

"Is there another way out of here?" I snapped.

He smiled. "No, there isn't."

The pounding at the door was getting louder. It sounded like they were using a battering ram against it.

I looked around the room, finally spotting a thick bundle of cables that ran up to the ceiling, then disappeared through a large grate.

"Everyone turn around and get down flat on the floor," I said.

They hesitated.

"Move it!"

Quickly they turned, got down on their hands and knees, and then lay down.

"Legs apart, hands clasped behind your head," I said as I dragged a chair over to a spot just beneath the cable opening in the ceiling.

The pounding at the door was getting louder now, coming in a regular pattern. They were definitely using something as a battering ram against it, and by the sound of it, the door would not last much longer.

I got up on the chair and shoved the grate upwards into the attic space where it fell over with a clatter.

One of the men on the floor looked up, and I pointed my pistol at him. He turned back, face down, his body rigid. I'm sure he expected me to shoot him at any moment.

Quickly I stuffed my Luger back in my parka pocket, pulled out the gas bomb, triggered it, then threw it down on the floor near the door. A second later I had swung up into the attic and pulled myself all the way through the opening.

The door finally burst open at the same moment the gas bomb went off with a dull pop, and I crawled away from the opening, stumbling over the thick cable runs, and banging my head painfully on the roof joists.

The siren continued, but the noise of pursuit subsided below in the communications center. They would be unconscious for at least six hours, and when they awoke they would have monumental headaches, and nausea that would last for days.

At the far end of the attic there was a ventilation grate which I kicked out without hesitation.

I was at the rear of the building. Across a narrow opening was another building, similar in size to this one, that appeared to be some kind of administrative center. Its windows were dark.

A pair of snowtracks, their engines howling, their headlights dancing, raced past along one of the side roads, and a moment later I crawled out of the ventilation hole and dropped the ten feet or so down to the snow.

Keeping low, I raced to the corner of the communications building and cautiously peered around it toward the front. There was a great deal of activity there. I could see at least a half dozen large snowtrack vehicles, and a number of cold-weather-suited men, all carrying rifles.

It was only going to take a couple of minutes for the gas I had released to dissipate, and once entry to the communications center was gained, and they found I had escaped through the attic, the search would widen. I was going to have to be gone before then if I was going to have any chance of getting back to the American base.

I turned and hurried back to the far corner of the communications building and peered around that side toward the front. There were more snowtrack vehicles and men on this side, making it impossible for me to make a run for it across either of the side streets.

Quickly I went across the back alley, looked in one of the windows of the Administration building, and seeing that it was an empty, darkened office, smashed the four layers of glass with my elbow. I didn't think anyone out front could hear the noise over the sounds of the snow-tracks, but I wasn't going to take any chances by going to see.

Within a few seconds I cleared away the jagged shards of glass and heaved myself up and threw the window into the office.

I took my Luger out of my pocket and hurried to the door to listen for any sounds outside. There was nothing, and I softly opened the door.

Just outside this office was a large room that contained a half dozen desks and dozens of file cabinets. The big room was dark and silent as well.

I hurried across it to another door from where I listened again. Still there was no noise from within the building, and I opened this door to a darkened corridor that stretched the length of the building, left and right.

A little longer, I told myself. Luck was running with me so far, I needed just a little more.

I stepped out into the corridor and walked silently toward the front of the building. The lights and sounds of the commotion outside came through the windows of what appeared to be a day room at the end of the corridor.

As I started across the room, I suddenly noticed a solitary figure silhouetted at a window, his back to me.

There was no one else in the room, I was sure of that. To my right was a set of stairs that led up to the second floor. To the left was a bulletin board and a large wall map of the Antarctic continent.

"Dmitri?" I said softly.

The figure at the window spun around. "Leonid. Is that you?"

"Da," I said, muffling my voice.

"Dmitri is gone, you motherless whore," the man said coming across the dark room toward me. "It's me, Yuri . . ."

Suddenly he stopped, realizing I wasn't who he thought I was.

"Do not cry out, Yuri, or you will die," I said evenly.

The man started to say something, but then clamped it off as he looked over his shoulder toward the window where he had been watching the goings-on across the street.

"Yes," I said. "They are looking for me. And if they find me, you will be the first to die."

"What do you want?" he said softly.

"A way out of here. Do you have access to a snow-track vehicle?"

"Out back," he said.

"Where is your parka?"

"Here," he said pointing toward one of the chairs, where a parka was draped over the back. "I just got up for the morning . . ." He cut it off.

"Get your coat then, Yuri, we are going for a ride. If you do exactly as I say, and try nothing fancy, you will live to tell your friends a very interesting story."

"Yes . . . yes," he said moving toward his coat. "I am a cook. I don't have a gun. I don't even know how to use a gun."

"That's just as well," I said.

He got his coat and pulled it on. "My machine is out back. Down the corridor."

I stepped aside, and waved my Luger that way. "You first. I'll be right behind you."

Yuri the cook hurried past me, then down the cor-

ridor to the other side of the building, away from the
activity outside.

"Where do you want me to take you?" he asked at the
outside door.

"The American base."

"That's fifty miles away," he said.

"That's right."

He half turned around to me. "My machine . . . it is
nothing more than a little snowmobile. It will never
make it. It does not carry fuel."

"Damn," I swore. "Where on this base can we get a
larger vehicle?"

"They are everywhere."

"One that wouldn't be attended. Be quick."

"The maintenance shop. I don't think anyone would
be there now," he said quickly, eyeing my gun.

"Then that's where we're going." I motioned toward
the door.

Yuri turned, opened the door, and we went outside to
where his small snowmobile was parked next to the
building. He climbed on behind the steering yoke, and I
climbed on behind him, the barrel of my Luger jammed
into his back.

"I do not want to kill you, Yuri, and I will not if you
make no mistakes."

He started the snowmobile without a word and
lurched the clutch on take-off. We went around the corner and headed down the street, the snarl of the small
engine all but lost to the still heavy wind.

Soon we were across the base from the lights and activity at the communications center, and Yuri turned
down a wide street that led directly toward the airstrip
and maintenance buildings. The white light on top of
one of the buildings marking the runway flashed on and
off in the night. Other than that, there was no other

movement on or around the airfield.

The road curved around in front of the maintenance buildings. The airstrip itself plowed through the snow and ice to the left. Several helicopters and two large transport aircraft were tied down on the apron.

Yuri pulled up and parked in front of the last building in a row and looked over his shoulder at me.

"This is where they repair the snowtracks," he said. "There should be a machine here that you can use."

I climbed off the snowmobile and motioned for Yuri to come with me. He shut off his machine and dismounted.

"I don't want to die," he said. He was on the verge of tears.

"And you won't, Yuri, if you continue to cooperate with me."

"I don't know for sure if there are machines in here," he said.

"We'll just go inside and see," I said, motioning him toward the building.

He turned and walked stiff-legged up to the front door of the building and went inside. I was right behind him.

Just through the door I groped for and found the light switch and flipped it on. The place was definitely a maintenance garage for snowtrack vehicles, and there were at least a dozen of them here. But not any vehicle was in one piece. Engine cowlings were off all the machines; some of them were missing their tracks; two of them were engineless; and parts and tools were scattered around all of them.

Yuri was looking back and forth from the machines to me, his mouth open, his eyes wide. I reached back and flipped the light switch off.

"Let's go," I said edging back to the door. I turned

and opened the door and looked outside. At that moment Yuri bolted deeper into the building, ducking around one of the large snowtrack vehicles.

For just a moment I debated going after him, but then decided against it. There wasn't enough time. Very soon now the troops from the communications center were going to come looking for me.

I stepped outside into the freezing cold, pocketed my Luger, and climbed on Yuri's snowmobile. The key was not in the ignition.

A siren sounded back on the base, and in the distance I could see the headlights of at least a dozen snowtrack machines, all heading this way. My luck, which had held up pretty well until this point, was just about to run out.

I got off the snowmobile and headed across to the building next to the maintenance garage. Just inside the front door was a day room, a corridor beyond that. Another administrative center, or perhaps a barracks.

Back outside, I hurried to the next building in the row, this one with large, service doors out front. It looked like a hangar for small aircraft, or helicopters.

A light was shining over a smaller door to the left, and as I stepped inside, the first of the snowtrack vehicles from the base screamed up the curved road around the airstrip.

The building was a hangar. In the dim light shining from overhead, I could see two helicopters parked in the middle. One of the machines was partially dismantled, its engine in pieces. The other machine, however, seemed intact.

The snowtracks were passing outside now, as I headed across to the intact helicopter. Near the back of the building was a set of stairs leading up to a series of doors. It was possible, I thought, that this building was not only a hangar but was also a pilot's ready center.

Reaching the small helicopter, I opened the door and looked inside. The machine seemed to be ready to fly. The keys were still in the ignition.

I reached inside and flipped on the master switch.

The gyro equipment on the instrument panel whined into life, the battery indicator came up, and the fuel gauges read full on both tanks. The machine *was* ready to fly. All I needed now was a pilot.

I hurried away from the machine, and took the stairs up two at a time, as more snowtrack vehicles screamed by the building.

At the top, I took out my Luger and approached the first door, where I listened. There was no sound from within, so I opened the door.

The room was deserted, although it was equipped with a bed, a desk and chair, and a closet.

The next two rooms were empty as well, but at the fourth room someone was asleep in the bed, and when I opened the door he sat up.

"What is it?" he mumbled.

I stepped the rest of the way into the small room, closing the door behind me, and raised my gun.

"Are you a helicopter pilot, comrade?" I asked softly.

"Of course I am. What the hell do you think . . ." he started to say, but then he realized I was holding a gun on him.

"Make any noise, and you will die," I said urgently.

"Who are you? What do you want here?" he said softly.

"I'm an American. I want to get back to my base."

"How did you get here?"

"Never mind," I snapped. "I want you to get up now and get dressed. You are going to fly me back to my base."

"Like hell I am."

I raised my Luger a little higher. "Then I will kill you."

The pilot smiled. "If you kill me, you'll never get out of here."

"It will not be your worry after that, although they'd probably send your medal to your family."

"All right . . . all right," the pilot said after a brief hesitation. He flipped the covers back and got out of bed. "You've got yourself a pilot. Now all you need is a machine."

"There's one downstairs."

He shook his head. "This is a maintenance hangar. The engine is apart on all of the birds down there. The other one was just brought in yesterday for work. It won't hold its oil pressure."

"We're taking it anyway."

"You're crazy. The engine would seize up within a few minutes."

"You'd better pray it doesn't, comrade, because we're flying out of here on that machine."

"No . . ."

I stepped quickly across the room and jammed the barrel of my Luger just below his chin. "I'm a desperate man, comrade. I *will* blow your head off. Now!"

The pilot's eyes went wide. "Yes . . . yes . . . I will do as you say."

I stepped back. "Get dressed. Hurry."

He was fully dressed in his cold weather gear within five minutes. I edged over to the door and opened it a crack. The hangar was ablaze with lights; below, there were at least half a dozen armed troops.

I stepped away from the door and motioned for the pilot to step out on the balcony. "They're looking for me down there," I whispered. "Get rid of them."

The pilot hesitated again.

"Don't be a hero, comrade. If I am discovered here, I will kill you first."

He nodded, then stepped past me and out to the balcony. "What's going on down there?" he shouted.

The beams of several strong lights suddenly centered on the pilot. "Are you alone up there?"

"No," the pilot shouted. "I have four women with me."

Someone laughed from below.

"Have them open the hangar doors," I whispered from within his room.

"One of you fellows open the doors down there for me," he shouted down.

"Why?"

"Because I don't want to fly my machine through them while they are closed, you idiot," the pilot shouted.

Someone else laughed. "What about your women, comrade?"

The doors rumbled open a few seconds later.

"No one here, Captain," someone said from below.

"What are you doing here at this hour?" the pilot shouted down.

But no one answered him, and a few seconds later I could hear several snowtrack machines starting up, then roaring away.

"Everyone gone?" I asked.

"Looks like it," the pilot said.

"Then let's go," I said. I stepped out of the room and followed him along the walkway, then down the stairs.

The hangar was deserted, and now that the service doors were open it was bitterly cold. We crossed quickly over to the helicopter where the pilot untied the rotors, then grabbed a couple of cans of oil, opened them, and put them in the engine.

I stood back behind the machine so that I would not be seen from the open doors. As the pilot worked, several snowtrack vehicles roared past on the road.

"They must want you very badly," the pilot said as he finished buttoning up the engine cowling.

"If they get me, they'll get you," I said. "Let's go."

The pilot came back around the machine. "We'll never make it all the way to your base."

"We'll try," I said.

He climbed aboard as I hurried around to the passenger side, then climbed up and strapped myself in.

The pilot started the engine and began going through his check list as a snowtrack pulled up by the open hangar doors and four men got out.

"No time," I snapped. "We're leaving now."

The pilot looked at me, then back outside at the four troops, all of them carrying rifles and heading in a dead run toward us.

He opened the throttle wide, and the helicopter leaped forward, rising a few inches up off the floor.

One of the troops was raising his rifle as we flashed past him, and outside the pilot cranked the rotors on full pitch, and we rose up into the night sky, the wind slamming us to the left, nearly causing us to hit the edge of the building. And then we were up, rising rapidly away from the Soviet installation, the red warning light on the engine oil indicator dial already blinking.

CHAPTER TEN

Within a couple of minutes or so we had cleared the Soviet base, and within five minutes we could no longer even see the rotating beacon that marked the airstrip.

The sky was still overcast, and there was nothing to see outside the bubble canopy except the blowing wind and snow straight ahead, and the vague outlines of the ice hills and hummocks a couple of hundred feet below.

I had turned off the communications radio almost immediately, and now as we flew I turned it back on and switched to the American base channel.

"We're too low and have not covered enough distance yet to pick up anything," the pilot said.

"How about the navigational aid transmitter?"

"That's what I'm following," he said. He reached out and turned up the volume on his navigation receiver, and I could hear the steady morse-code beeping of our homing beacon.

"How soon before we're in range of the communications radio?" I asked.

The pilot shook his head. "We're not going to get that far, I've already told you." He pointed at the engine temperature gauge which was well up into the red. "The engine is going to seize up at any moment."

Another ten or fifteen minutes and we would have

made it all the way, but even as I looked down at the
forbidding landscape we were passing over, the
helicopter's engine began to slow down.

"Let me set down here before it's too late. I can key
our emergency locator beacon, and my people will pick
us up within ten or fifteen minutes."

"If I'm captured your people will kill me," I said.
There was no reason to lie to him.

"For what?" he snapped. "What have you done?"

"Not a thing. As a matter of fact I'm trying to stop
something from happening."

The needle on the engine temperature gauge was
pegged to the right now, and the smell of hot oil and
overheated metal began to fill the cabin.

There was no way we were going to make it anywhere
near the American base.

"How far out are we now?"

"I don't know for sure," the pilot said. He cranked in
full power to the rotors, but the engine did not want to
respond as it continued to overheat and the RPMs continued to drop. "Fifteen maybe twenty miles from my
base . . ." he started to add, when a large, sickening
bang came from behind us in the engine.

A buzzer sounded on the panel, and the pilot looked
over his shoulder. "Fire," he said. With one hand on the
control column, he reached out with his other and
flipped the fire extinguisher switch, then he started to
reach beneath his seat for the emergency locator transmitter, but I grabbed his hand and shoved it aside.

"They'll never find us," he shouted.

"We'll walk the rest of the way."

"You're crazy . . . we're not equipped to cross thirty
miles in these conditions . . ."

The helicopter lurched to the left at that moment, and
then dove toward the ice.

I braced myself for the crash, and at the last moment the pilot managed to bring the nose of the helicopter up so that we came in tail first.

We slammed over to the right, then flipped upside down on the pilot's side, the bubble canopy shattering and collapsing.

Something smashed into my shoulder as the machine seemed to crumple inward on itself, and then I was lying half in and half out of the machine, my face in the snow.

Slowly, painfully, I reached back and somehow managed to unstrap my seat belt, then crawled out of the wreckage where I rolled over on my back.

The pilot was obviously dead, his body crushed beneath the heavy engine and engine mounts. Aviation fuel was spilling everywhere, and over the noise of the wind I could hear the loud ticking from the still hot engine.

I rolled over, got to my feet and stumbled away from the machine, which caught on fire almost immediately. About fifty yards away I stopped and turned back to watch as the remaining fuel in the gas tank exploded with a dull whump, sending flames shooting fifty feet into the night air.

If I had had any hope of salvaging something that could help me from the wreckage, the fire had made that impossible. I was on my own now, probably at least thirty miles away from the American base at McMurdo Sound. Thirty miles of the most inhospitable territory in the entire world. Meanwhile Stalnov was inland at our installation, and a Soviet submarine was forty-eight hours away from a rendezvous along the coast.

I turned and faced the direction we had been traveling. My chances were almost nil. I knew it. And yet I could not remain here and wait to die. I had to try.

After a moment, I tightened the draw strings on my

parka hood, and headed away from the helicopter, walking through the deep snow as fast as I could go.

As long as I managed to keep going I would survive. If I stopped, I would die. It was as simple as that.

The flames from the burning helicopter behind me were finally starting to die down as I topped a rise about a mile away, stopped, and looked back.

It had seemed to me like I had been walking for hours, and yet I was only a mile from where we had crashed. Only one mile.

I shook my head and was about to turn away, when I caught a pair of winking lights beyond the wreckage. Then I lost them.

For a long moment I stared in the direction where I thought I had seen the lights, and then I saw them again. Much closer now, and lower.

The noise of a helicopter engine finally came to me over the wind, and instinctively I hunched down in the snow as I watched the machine come in low over the wrecked helicopter, then touch down just beyond it.

In the light from the flames, I could just make out the silhouettes of several figures darting from the helicopter that had just arrived—no doubt from the Soviet base.

As I watched, a second, and then a third helicopter came into view. One of them touched down, while the other hovered nearby, shining a bright spotlight down around the wreckage.

It wouldn't take them very long to realize there was only one body in the machine. And from the looks of things, I didn't think they would just let me wander around out here.

They evidently knew, or at least guessed who I was and had to assume that since I had made it to the communications center, I now knew about the submarine and why it was coming.

The fact that the Russians were going all out to stop me was as good as an admission from them of what Paul Tibert had suspected.

I turned and headed away in a shambling run made difficult because of the deep snow and the biting wind. But a plan was beginning to form in my mind. A desperate gamble it would be; but having crossed only one mile of this terrain, I knew that my chances of actually making it back to the American base on foot were an even wilder gamble.

First, however, I was going to have to put as much distance between me and the wrecked helicopter as possible. The farther away I got, the more their search efforts would have to spread out, and therefore the farther apart each of the searching helicopters would be from each other.

Beyond the rise where I had stopped, the ice and snow sloped sharply down into the darkness. For a few moments I wondered if I wasn't on the side of some kind of a mountain. I had no way of knowing whether or not this slope would steepen and turn into a precipice over which I would fall.

Yet to turn around and go back was to invite almost certain capture and death.

I had a chance and I meant to take it, no matter what the risk was.

The terrain continued to slope downward, sometimes at a gentle angle, at other times steeper. But after at least another mile, I began to realize that I was on an undulating plane of ice and snow that probably stretched all the way up the coast to the American base.

At the next rise I stopped long enough to turn back and search the darkness behind me. I could vaguely make out the lights of one of the helicopters far to my right—but nothing else.

They had already started their search. They knew now that I had survived the crash and was out here somewhere.

I continued down the next slope, stumbling almost immediately and tumbling end over end at least fifty yards down to the bottom.

I was shaken but not hurt. After a moment, when I had caught my breath, I started to get up when I heard the noise of a helicopter very close overhead, and I slumped back down.

It was going to happen now. I had hoped to put a little more distance between myself and the downed helicopter, but it was too late to worry about it.

The helicopter flashed very low over me, the downdraft from its rotors kicking up a huge plume of snow and an incredibly cold wind.

It was back a few seconds later, hovering a few yards behind me as its spotlight probed the darkness, finally centering on my prone figure.

The cold was seeping through my body, at times making it almost impossible to think.

The helicopter finally set down somewhere behind me, and within a minute or so I was being turned over on my back, a strong light in my eyes.

I mumbled something incoherent as one of the men searched me, coming up with my Luger. A moment later two of them were helping me to my feet, but I let my body go limp so that they had to drag me back to the helicopter.

"It's the American," one of them shouted.

"Is he disarmed?" someone else called back from inside the helicopter as we approached it.

"I have his gun," the one on my right said.

Then they were helping me in the back seat of the helicopter, strapping me in, and I let my head fall forward as I continued to mumble.

"Red leader one, this is unit two, we have him," the pilot said.

"Be careful with him Vasily. He is dangerous," the radio blared.

"We have his weapon, and he is only semi-conscious," the pilot radioed.

"Bring him directly to Admin One. We're heading back now."

"Yes, sir," the pilot said.

Everyone had gotten into the helicopter, and, as we lifted off, I opened my eyes a crack.

There was one man seated next to me; in the front the pilot sat in the left seat, and the co-pilot in the right. As far as I could tell there was no one else aboard.

I felt bad about the death of the pilot I had forced to fly with me away from the Soviet base, and about the fact there was a very good chance that one or more of these men would possibly die, but this was war. They had already killed thirty-one people out at our research site. They meant to kill me, and they were planning on transporting the deadly RVB-A back to Moscow. No matter what else occurred, I could not let that happen.

The helicopter lurched into a small airpocket. At that moment I popped open my seatbelt and fell all the way forward, I slipped my stiletto out of its sheath, gripping it lightly in my right hand.

The man seated next to me came forward to grab me, but I bunched up my left fist and hit him twice in rapid succession in his face. His head snapped back, bouncing against the rear frame of the helicopter.

The co-pilot was starting to swivel around in his seat, bringing around his service revolver. I sat forward again and quickly brought the point of my razor sharp stiletto up to the pilot's neck.

"Drop your weapon or the pilot dies!" I shouted.

The co-pilot hesitated, his revolver just level with the top of the seat back.

"Do as I say, comrade, I do not want us all to die," I said.

The co-pilot finally nodded and started to turn forward.

"Here in the back," I said. "I want your weapon."

The man seated next to me was unconscious. The co-pilot glanced at him, then slowly reached over the top of his seat and dropped his gun on the floor at my feet.

Shifting the stiletto to my left hand, but keeping the point against the pilot's neck, I reached down and grabbed the Russian's pistol, then quickly sat back.

"The gun is pointed at the pilot's back," I said. "But if you do exactly as I tell you, no one will get hurt."

"What do you want?" the pilot finally asked.

I reached over to my right and took the unconscious man's weapon, as well as my Luger.

"I want you to turn immediately to a heading that will take us to the American base. Do it now."

The pilot and co-pilot looked at each other, but then the helicopter banked to the right, straightening out after a long, sweeping turn.

"Now turn your radio to the American frequency."

After a slight hesitation, the co-pilot switched the radio frequency.

"Give me the microphone," I said. "Carefully."

The co-pilot passed the mike back to me, and I brought it to my lips and keyed it.

"McMurdo Sound, McMurdo Sound, this is Captain Carter, do you copy?"

There was nothing from the speaker except static crashes.

"Give me a little more altitude," I said.

The pilot brought us up.

I keyed the mike. "McMurdo Sound, McMurdo Sound, this is Captain Carter, do you copy, over?"

"This is McMurdo Sound," an American voice came over the speaker. "Say again your identification."

"McMurdo, this is Captain Nick Carter. I am part of the commission with Commander Paul Tibert."

"That's a roger, Captain. We've been trying for the last twelve hours to raise you. What's your status, and is Commander Tibert there with you?"

"Negative, negative," I said. "Now listen to me very closely. I am presently aboard a Soviet helicopter, about twenty miles down the coast from you. I have the pilot and co-pilot at gunpoint. A third crew-member is unconscious for the moment. We're going to land right in the middle of the airstrip. I want an armed escort out there to meet us."

There was a long pause on the radio. Then another voice came on. "Carter, is this some kind of a joke?"

"Negative, negative," I snapped. "I want an armed guard there to meet us, as well as a fuel truck. I'm sending them back as soon as they drop me off. Do you understand?"

"Aye aye, Captain, but I hope to hell you're kidding about this."

"I'm not. Now get the lead out, our ETA is . . ." I released the microphone switch, and in Russian asked the pilot our ETA. He told me nine minutes. "Nine minutes. You copy?"

"That's a roger. We have you on radar."

I tossed the microphone back up front. "No tricks now, gentlemen. We're going to set down in the middle of our airstrip where an armed guard will be waiting for us. I'm going to get out; your machine will be refueled, courtesy of the U.S. Navy, and then you will be allowed to return to your base. Have I made myself clear?"

"*Da,*" the pilot said. The co-pilot nodded his head.

We flew then for the next few minutes in silence, until the co-pilot stiffened. I sat forward. Through the forward canopy I could just make out the lights of our base.

"Nice and easy now," I cautioned.

The pilot glanced at his partner in the right seat, and they both nodded. "Captain Carter," the pilot said.

"What?"

"I . . . we, do not want to return."

"What are you saying to me?"

"We don't want to go back to our base," the co-pilot said.

"Are you defecting? Is that what you're telling me?"

The co-pilot nodded.

"How about your friend here in back with me?"

"He will come with us," the pilot said. He glanced again at the co-pilot. "We have talked about this before."

We were coming up on the lighted airstrip very fast now. This could be some kind of a trick on their part, but somehow I didn't think so.

"Bring us down carefully," I said.

"We don't want to go back," the pilot said.

"I'll have to think about it. But it's going to depend on how well you cooperate with me," I said. "Do you understand?"

"*Da,*" both men said.

We came in low over the airstrip a couple of minutes later. Below I could see half a dozen snowtracks, at least fifteen men standing around them, while twenty yards away a fuel truck was just pulling up.

The pilot set the helicopter down directly in the middle of the runway, then shut the engine off, and we were surrounded by armed men, their weapons up and at the ready.

I popped open the door. "It's me, Captain Carter," I shouted.

"Out of the helicopter very slowly," one of the troops shouted back.

"Let's go," I said.

"Will you help us?" the pilot asked.

"A step at a time, comrade, and then I'll see."

We got slowly out of the helicopter, the co-pilot opening the rear door on his side, helping the still unconscious man outside.

One of the Navy officers I had met with Tibert came up to me, an amazed, incredulous expression on his face.

"Jesus H. Christ, it *is* you," he said. "Where in the hell did you come from?"

"The Soviet installation down the coast," I said.

"How—" he started to sputter, but I cut him off.

"There's no time to explain now," I snapped. "I want this helicopter secured out of sight. I want these three men brought to a room I can use for interrogation. I want a doctor to look at one of them. I think his nose is broken. You can feed them too. Finally I need to use the communications center immediately. You can bring me something to eat there."

The officer was staring gape mouthed at me. "Any thing else, Captain?"

"Yeah," I said, "I want a package of cigarettes and a bottle of brandy. Now let's move it, we don't have a hell of a lot of time."

The officer stared at me a moment longer, then shook his head. "All right, you heard the man. A-crew, I want this bird secured. Smitty, take a couple of men and bring these troops over to the staff conference room in Admin and get them looked after and fed." He turned to me. "I'll take you to the Comm center myself."

I followed him to a snowtrack vehicle where we

climbed aboard and took off across the field. "Now, can you tell me what the hell is going on, Captain? Like for starters, where Commander Tibert is?"

"Paul Tibert is dead," I said. "He was murdered."

"My God, what the hell is going on here?"

"How many armed men do you have here?" I asked. He looked at me. "Twenty-two. You just saw all of them."

"No other weapons?"

"They're mostly scientists down here."

"This installation may come under attack within the next hour or so," I said, my words like bombshells to the man. "Have your radar watchers keep a sharp lookout toward the Soviet base."

"This can't be happening."

"It is," I said. "They'll be coming after me."

"You . . ."

"But I'm going to be gone within an hour. I'll need a good snowtrack, a couple of your rifles and ammunition, food, survival gear, a good radio transceiver, and some kind of radio direction-finding equipment so I can get back out to the research installation."

"What's going on, Captain? Who killed Commander Tibert, the Russians?"

We had come to the communications center. "I have to get a message off to Washington. While I'm doing that, I want you to get the things I asked for. Then I'm going to want to talk to the three Russians. Afterwards, if there's time, I'll explain everything."

The officer finally nodded. "Fair enough. But I hope to hell you're wrong about all this."

"Me, too," I said. But I wasn't.

CHAPTER ELEVEN

Lieutenant Commander Bob Theisen buzzed the Crypto Section door within the communications center, and it was opened a second later by a young ensign, a startled expression on his face.

We brushed past him all the way into the cramped room that was filled with encryption equipment, and half a dozen teletype machines along one wall.

"This is Captain Carter. He's with Naval Intelligence. Top clearance. Give him whatever he needs."

"Aye aye, sir," the ensign said, eyeing me with uncertainty.

Theisen turned to me. "I can be back here with your things within a half hour. Will that give you enough time?"

"Plenty," I said. "But you'd better get your people together, as well as a civilian representative or two. As soon as I finish talking with the three men I brought in, I'll brief you all."

"Are they going to start a shooting war down here?" he asked.

"I don't think so, not unless you offer them more than a passive resistance. Once they find out that I've gone, they'll back off." I looked around at the equipment.

"When I'm finished here you'd better be ready to destroy this stuff."

"What the hell—" the young ensign started to say.

"Do whatever this man says," Theisen snapped, and he turned on his heel and left.

"What have you got in the way of a secured line to the Pentagon?" I asked.

"Two, sir," the young man said. "One is a data link, the other is teletype."

"Are you passing any traffic on the teletype circuit at this moment?"

He looked over his shoulder at one of the clattering machines. "Yes, sir," he said.

"Pull it off then. I'll need a clear line. I'll write down the routing indicators for you."

"Can you tell me what's going on, sir?"

"Get me that clear line," I said. "When I'm finished here, I'll want you to destroy your equipment, then get the hell out of here. Go on back to your barracks, and stay there."

"Yes, sir," he said, and he turned and went back to one of the pieces of equipment, flipped a couple of switches, then went to the teletype that suddenly went quiet.

I grabbed a blank message form from the desk and quickly wrote out the routing indicators that would open circuits through the Pentagon, direct to AXE's Operations Room on Dupont Circle.

The ensign had established manual contact with his counterpart in the Pentagon's Crypto Center when I handed him the routings.

"Tell him the first four digits are for his Tech Control. They'll bring up the right circuit," I said.

The ensign looked up at me and nodded. He was shaken up, but he sent the routing instructions I had written out for him, and seconds later the teletype chattered out four Xs, and then four bells, followed by the word: READY.

"All right, Ensign," I said. "Go get yourself a cup of coffee."

"Yes, sir," he said scrambling out of the chair.

I sat down at the teletype machine and typed: GIVE ME HAWK—N3 HERE."

"HAWK IS SUMMONED. BEGIN MESSAGE N3."

As quickly as I could type then, I reported everything that had happened since I had arrived here at McMurdo Sound, including Tibert's guess that the Soviets may have been trying to transport a supply of the deadly RVB-A they had developed here. I also reported the fact that a Soviet submarine was due to rendezvous off the Antarctic coast near Mt. Sabine in less than forty-eight hours.

Through all of that, which took me at least fifteen minutes, the young ensign remained perched on the edge of his desk across the room, an expression of intense worry on his face.

"MESSAGE RECEIVED," the reply came when I was finished. "HAWK HERE. WHAT IS YOUR BEST ESTIMATE OF THE SOVIETS' INTENTIONS AT THIS POINT?"

"THEY MUST MAKE RENDEZVOUS WITH THEIR SUB AT ALL COSTS. BELIEVE THEY MAY TAKE THIS INSTALLATION BY FORCE IN AN EFFORT TO FIND AND STOP ME."

"HOLD," the teletype clattered.

I sat back and lit myself a cigarette. I could envision the intense activity in AXE Operations at this moment, as our analysts worked out feasible game plans, and Hawk pulled the strings.

Ten minutes later the door buzzer sounded. The ensign got up and opened the door. Bob Theisen came in carrying what looked like a box lunch in one hand and a bottle of brandy in the other, which he left on the desk. Then he came over to me.

"All I could scratch up were some sandwiches," he said apologetically. "Breakfast is in about a half an hour if you'll have the time."

"Did you get everything else for me?" I asked.

He was staring down at the messages on the teletype machine. "Yeah," he said absently.

The teletype came to life again. "SOONEST WE CAN PROVIDE SUB-SURFACE BACKUP FROM MELBOURNE IS SIXTY HOURS. ICE PACK IN VICINITY PROHIBITS SURFACE VESSELS. BELIEVED AERIAL STRIKE WOULD NOT—RPT—WOULD NOT BE EFFECTIVE. CAN YOU STOP RENDEZVOUS—OR DELAY SAME UNTIL BACKUP ARRIVES? ADVISE."

Theisen had read my message and the replies, and now he whistled. "We don't have the troops," he said.

"AFFIRMATIVE," I typed.

"GOOD LUCK," the teletype printed.

I pulled the long message paper out of the machine, folded it a couple of times, and handed it to Theisen as I got up. "As of now this information is classified top secret. I want this destroyed immediately."

He took the paper to a portable shredder in one corner and ran it through the machine.

"Can I start the traffic now, sir?" the ensign asked.

I shook my head. "This place is probably going to be overrun by a Soviet assault team. They'll be looking for me, but they'll probably be instructed to grab whatever else they come across." Theisen looked at me. "You'd better destroy this equipment now, and then get back to your barracks and sit tight."

The ensign looked to Theisen, who nodded. I grabbed my box lunch and the bottle of brandy and headed to the door.

"Let's go," I snapped.

Theisen caught up with me outside where we climbed into the snowtrack vehicle he had brought for me. In back was the equipment and supplies I had requested.

"Have you got your people ready for my briefing?" I asked.

"They're in the conference room."

"All right. First I want to talk with the three Russians I brought in."

Theisen started the machine, then headed off across the base as I wolfed down a couple of the tasteless sandwiches and the chocolate bar. By the time I was finished with my brief meal, we had pulled up in front of the Administration building, where we went inside and directly to a small room just off Commander Tibert's office. A Navy guard was posted at the door.

"Anything from radar yet?" I asked just before we went inside.

"Nothing yet," Theisen said. "Maybe they won't be coming."

"They will," I said.

We went inside where the three Russians were seated around a small table. They were just finishing the same kind of box lunch I had just eaten, and someone had thought to provide them with a bottle of vodka, which they were sharing.

They all looked up, recognizing me immediately.

I sat down across the table from them, grabbed a clean glass, and poured myself a stiff shot of the brandy I had brought with me. Theisen remained standing by the door.

I would have to use these three men. I didn't like it but if they suspected that their people would be coming here to take over this base, they would not tell me a thing. They would behave as the captured enemy, not defectors.

They were going to have to be strung out on a limb, at least for the time being.

I drank the shot of brandy as they watched me, then set the glass down. "Before we decide what to do with you, I'm going to have to have some quick and honest answers," I said in Russian.

They nodded.

"It will be as you ask, Captain," the pilot said.

"Good," I said. "What do you know about the rendezvous of one of your submarines off the coast near Mt. Sabine?"

The three looked at each other. "Nothing," the pilot said. "I have heard of no such thing."

I felt he was telling me the truth. "Has anything unusual been happening on your base over the past few days?"

They all nodded. "There has been a great deal of activity recently," the co-pilot said. He was a young man, probably in his mid-twenties.

"What kind of activity?"

He shrugged. "Increased security. More marines. Many more armed men."

"The KGB has opened an office as well," the pilot added.

"No explanations?"

They all shook their heads.

"How about among the scientists?"

"There are very few scientific personnel left on the base," the pilot said, an odd expression on his face.

I sat forward. "What happened to them?"

"They all started leaving about one month ago. A few at a time, with no replacements coming in."

They had completed their research, after all. They evidently had manufactured enough of the RVB-A for all their needs. All they had to do now was to get the material back to the Soviet Union, and then use it. The implications were frightening.

I shook my head, poured myself another shot of the brandy, drank it down, and then got to my feet.

I felt bad for these three. They were in a very difficult position now. But they had given me what I believed to be the truth; I owed them the same.

"Gentlemen, I wish I could be more optimistic for you," I said in formal Russian. "But I cannot be. Your people want me very badly. It is my belief that a force of your marines will be coming to this base very soon. I will be gone by then. Back to New Zealand. But when they find you here . . ."

The three of them understood the implications, and their complexions turned pale.

"You have two choices now," I said. "You can remain with us and help with the resistance, or . . ." I looked over at Theisen, "Or, we can place you under arrest in one of our unheated buildings. You will be our unwilling prisoners. You can tell your people, when you are released, that you were interrogated harshly, but gave us no information. I would suggest that you give yourselves bloody noses, perhaps break out a few teeth, to make it a little more convincing."

They looked at each other.

"You can't let them go like that," Theisen said.

"Oh yes I can, and I will," I snapped.

"You would do this for us . . ." the pilot said.

I nodded. "I'm afraid it isn't much. But this is very important. It could mean a world war. And that, comrades, is the truth as far as I know it."

They looked at each other again. "Can we be given American uniforms?"

I nodded.

"It can be arranged," Theisen said.

"Then we will stay and take our chances with you," the pilot said.

"As you wish," I said, looking down at them. "But you must understand that you cannot be given weapons."

"We understand."

"Good luck, then," I said.

"And to you," the pilot replied.

Theisen and I left the interrogation room, where he gave instructions to one of his people to fix the Russians up with American uniforms and then get them out of the way.

"You're not going back to New Zealand, are you?" Theisen asked me before we went into the conference room.

I shook my head. "No. I'm going back out to the research installation. But I want you to ask for a couple of volunteers to fly back there."

"If all this is true, and the Russians believe you're on that aircraft, they might just shoot it down," Theisen said.

"That's why I want you to ask for volunteers," I said.

"Sixty hours," Theisen said.

"It's a long time. A lot can happen."

He nodded, and we went into the conference room where half a dozen men, two of them civilians, were seated around the conference table. It was the same room in which Commander Tibert had briefed the commission members before we went out to the installation.

Theisen started to make the introductions, but I cut him short.

"There's no time for that," I said. "It doesn't matter who you are. I'm Captain Nick Carter, Naval Intelligence. You may or may not know that I was part of the commission, under Commander Paul Tibert, that was formed to study the incident that occurred out at your research installation."

One of the civilians sat forward. "What are you doing back here, Captain? Are you finished out there? Have you discovered what happened?"

"Where is Commander Tibert?" another man asked.

"Commander Tibert is dead," I said.

"My God," the civilian said, sitting back. "Whatever killed them . . . it's still active?"

I waited for his words to die off. Everyone around the table was waiting for me to continue. They wanted an explanation.

"What I'm about to tell you is classified information, top secret, and I want you to treat the information with the utmost respect. Your lives, and the lives of everyone else on this base, could very well depend upon it. Have I made myself clear?"

"What is it?" the civilian asked.

Step by step I told them essentially the same things I had told David Hawk over the teletype circuit, including the business about the secret laboratory our people had maintained beneath the generator building, and Hawk's reply that help would not arrive until a full twelve hours after the Soviet submarine was due to rendezvous off the coast near Mt. Sabine.

When I finished, the men around the conference table were all silent—each immersed in his own thoughts and fears.

Finally, however, the civilian scientist who had spoken up at first stood up. "There is a lot of work to be done, then, before we're overrun."

Everyone else got up.

"How do you intend on stopping, or delaying, the Soviet submarine, Captain?" someone else asked.

I was on my feet. I shook my head. "Honestly . . . I don't know."

"I'd offer you my help, but I don't think it would amount to much. They didn't cover this in Biology 101."

Everyone chuckled, his comment serving to lighten the heavy mood.

"I don't think the Soviets mean you people any harm, provided you offer no more than an indignant resistance. But they're going to want me. It's very important that you convince them that I'm on my way to New Zealand."

"We'll do what we can, Captain," the scientist said, "but it's going to be up to you. God help you."

"Thank you," I said, for lack of anything else to say. And suddenly it struck me that what I was about to set out to try to do was totally impossible. Not only was a Soviet nuclear submarine due to appear off the bleak antarctic coast, but it was going to be met by a large, well armed, and very determined force of men who believed just as strongly in their country and her ideals as I did in mine.

I was going to be one man against that. It seemed impossible. And yet I'd been faced with impossible odds before, and always seemed to manage. Yet this time I did not have the same confidence that I usually have. I had been incredibly lucky so far on this assignment; I wondered just how much longer I could push it.

Theisen and I left the conference room and headed through the Administration section to the main door, where my snowtrack was waiting.

"If they get wind of the fact that you're on your way back out to the installation, they'll stop you," he said.

I nodded. "What's the weather look like?"

"Clear for the next twenty-four hours, but there's another front developing about a hundred miles out in the Ross Sea."

At the door we stopped, and Theisen looked directly into my eyes. "What about the others out at the installation. What has happened to them?"

I had put all thought of them in the back of my mind, until now. "I don't know for sure," I said. "But Stalnov is out there watching them. As long as they haven't tried to get away, I think they'll be all right."

"I hope so," Theisen said.

"COMMANDER THEISEN, COMMANDER THEISEN, CALL 315, CALL 315," blared a loudspeaker over the door.

Theisen turned, went back into the Administration center, and picked up one of the phones and dialed the number.

He spoke on the phone for just a few seconds, and when he hung up he looked very worried.

"You were right," he said to me.

"Radar?"

He nodded. "They've picked up at least a dozen large aircraft heading this way from the direction of the Soviet installation down the coast."

"All right, Bob, I'm getting out of here now while I still can. Get an aircraft off as soon as you possibly can."

"Get going," Theisen snapped, and he dialed another number.

"Good luck," I said, but he didn't hear me as he began relaying frantic orders.

I left the Administration building, climbed aboard the snowtrack, started the engine, and headed down the freshly plowed street toward the track that led away from the base.

It was just starting to get light out. But the day would last only a couple of hours down here at this time of the year, which was fine with me. I needed all the cover I could get.

Once the Soviets realized I was not on the base, they would have to assume I had either left aboard the aircraft on its way to New Zealand, or was on my way back out to the installation.

I only hoped that I would have at least a couple of hours headstart before they started looking for me. And I also hoped that no one would get hurt here on the base.

Within a few minutes I had passed the last few buildings on the base, then headed at top speed out along the cleared path inland. The machine bucked and heaved over the uneven snowdrifts and ice hummocks as the terrain rose up away from the coast.

I hoped to be over at least the first series of ice hills before the Soviet aircraft arrived over the base. If I could get that far, I would have a better than even chance of making it all the way without detection.

Beyond that, it was anyone's guess what was going to happen.

CHAPTER TWELVE

Over the first hill, about two miles from the base, I got out of the snowtrack and walked back up to the crest. From there I could see the entire base spread out below me.

The C130 I had come down here aboard had taxied out to the end of the runway, its huge propellers kicking up long plumes of snow.

It turned slowly, lumbered out to the center of the runway, and then began accelerating as the first of the large Soviet helicopters came into view.

Two of the Russian machines headed directly for the Hercules, and for a few terrible moments I was convinced that they meant to shoot the transport out of the sky.

But then the C130 was lifting off, climbing as it banked to the right, and the Soviet helicopters began landing on the runway near the Administration building.

I waited another few minutes as our troops came out to meet the Soviet forces that had emerged from the half a dozen helicopters. But there was no shooting. The Russian force was overwhelmingly larger than ours, and I imagined that Theisen was stalling for time with all the usual protests.

Back in the snowtrack I headed away from the coast, the radio direction finder providing me with a reciprocal bearing from the McMurdo Sound base to the research installation.

At first the terrain rose in a series of gentle hills, but finally it flattened out to a gently undulating plain of ice and snow, the crevasse detector pinging its warning almost immediately.

I pulled up short and opened the map that Theisen had given me. The track out to the research installation was clearly marked through this and two other crevasse regions, with the proper RDF bearings in brackets.

Laying the map on the seat next to me, I turned to the new course and continued slowly for the next couple of miles, following the serpentine track through the band of deep cracks in the ice cap.

Within half an hour I had safely crossed the region, and once again I turned back to a direct course out to the installation, and sped up.

The sun, which had just peeked above the horizon for a brief period of daylight, set, plunging the terrain into a darkness made deeper by the steadily increasing clouds of the approaching storm.

I stopped more frequently now to take RDF bearings. By the time I reached the next crevasse region I was going to have to be right on track, or I would not be able to find the pre-plotted way through the area.

Once I thought I spotted winking aircraft lights in the distance to my left, and I stopped and hurriedly switched the headlights off—and waited.

If it was an aircraft, however, the crew had not spotted me, because it never reappeared.

I waited a full fifteen minutes before I turned the headlights back on and continued along my course, the overcast thickening, blotting out all the stars now, the wind beginning to rise once again.

It was late at night, well after midnight, when I finally passed through the last crevasse region less than ten miles from the research installation.

I was dead tired, my eyes burning, my muscles aching. It seemed like it had been a year since I had slept last, and yet I could not afford to stop and rest now. Not until I made sure everything was all right back at the installation.

At one point I had debated using the radio to try and contact the base camp back at McMurdo Sound, but decided against it. If the Soviets were still on the base and intercepted my communication, they would be out here within the hour. In force.

Down the front side of the last hill, I came up behind the generator building, passed the downed radio tower, where Tibert's body still lay, and pulled up in front of the Administration building.

There was no light coming from any of the windows, but at first I thought nothing of it. I figured everyone was probably asleep.

I shut off the snowtrack, grabbed the portable radio from the back, and pushed my way through the deep snow to the front door.

A stiff breeze was blowing now, and the temperature had plunged to at least fifty below; the main thrust of the storm, however, was not due to hit for another dozen hours or so. When it did finally hit, however, all outside activity would come to a halt—ours as well as the Russians. It would give me time to catch up on some much needed rest.

I pulled open the door and stepped inside the day room. It was dark. And cold. For a long moment I just stood there listening to the wind outside, feeling the penetrating iciness of the day room.

Slowly then, I set the radio down on the floor and groped for the light switch, flicking it on when I found it. But nothing happened. The electricity was off. The place was dead.

"Stalnov!" I shouted into the darkness as I pulled out my Luger.

There was no answer.

"Lana!" I shouted. "Abel! Jean-Père!"

The only sound was the wind moaning through the eaves outside.

I went outside and grabbed a large flashlight out of the snowtrack and snapped it on. There were a great number of footprints in the snow around the front door, and a few yards away were the deep, ribbed depressions of several snowtrack machines, leading off to the west.

The Russians had been here. They had moved in, probably on Stalnov's signal, and had taken over this installation.

I turned and looked at the door. They had either taken everyone away, or they had killed all of them.

If I had stayed this would not have happened. Or if I had taken Stalnov with me, the entire thing could have been resolved hours ago.

The Soviet submarine would be at its rendezvous within thirty-six hours. Our sub out of Melbourne, would arrive ten hours after that.

There was time, I told myself as I started across to the generator building. There was still time.

It took me at least twenty minutes inside the dark, cold generator building to realize that the Russians had done nothing more than turn off the generators.

The batteries were nearly frozen, and the big diesel generator did not want to start. But I held down on the starter switch, the batteries grinding, until the big diesel finally coughed into life, threatened to quit, then settled down to a steady roar.

Outside, I hurried as quickly as I could back past my snowtrack to the front door of the Administration building, and went inside.

The light switch worked this time. Lying by the doorway to the corridor that led back to the dining hall was Bates-Wilcox, the British microbiologist. He had been shot at least half a dozen times. Frozen blood was splattered all around him. Clasped in his right hand was a .45 automatic.

I crossed the room to his body and pried the automatic from his grasp. The weapon had not been fired. The safety was still on. He had not had a chance.

"Lana!" I shouted.

The heater fan clicked on, and I could feel a warm blast of air from the grille near the doorway. I shoved my parka hood back, stepped over Bates-Wilcox's body, and slowly walked down the corridor.

At least a hundred brass shell casings littered the floor near the doorway to the dining hall. I bent down and picked up one of them. It was a 30 caliber shell. Odd.

Tossing the casing aside I stepped around the corner into the dining hall. Bullet holes pockmarked the walls and ceiling. In the middle of the room one of the long tables was turned up on its edge, the top riddled with bullet holes.

I stepped all the way into the room, the pungent odor of re-perked coffee coming from the kitchen area, and carefully made my way to the table.

Dr. Kurt Abel, the West German geneticist, was crouched in a heap on his knees, the top of his head blown away. He had no weapon.

I stepped backwards, my boots crunching on broken dishes.

Stalnov and his people had done this. But there had been no real reason for it. The Soviets had wanted to make sure their rendezvous with the submarine went without a hitch. These scientists, isolated out here without a radio, couldn't have done a thing about it. So why had they been killed? Why?

There was no one in the kitchen, the radio room, or the offices, although it was obvious that someone had been there searching for something.

My first big surprise came in the living quarters where I found Dr. Peter Straub's body. The East German had evidently been trying to pry open the window of his room when he had been shot down.

The second big surprise—the biggest, most disconcerting surprise of all—came near the rear door of the housing wing, where I discovered Stalnov's bullet-riddled body.

The door was open a crack, his frozen hand jutting outside, his body ripped apart by at least a dozen bullet wounds.

I dragged him back into the corridor and shut the door, then stared down at his body.

They had overrun this installation. But why had they killed one of their own people? It didn't make much sense. No matter how much of a threat they considered this commission to be, why kill one of their own people? Why kill Straub, one of their allies?

Over the next hour and a half I worked my way, room by room, through the rest of the buildings. Elsie de Hoorn's body, along with the bodies of the twenty-seven installation scientists and the bodies of the helicopter pilot and crewman, were laid out in the pathology lab. But the Frenchman Jean-Père, the Chinese physician Tien Sing, and Lana Edwards were nowhere to be found.

Back at the dining hall I stopped once again to pick up one of the shell casings. It, too, was a 30 caliber. But the Russians did not use that caliber weapon.

I hurried down the corridor, across the day room, and outside; then I trudged across the snow to the generator building.

When I had been here to start the generator, I had not stopped to check the secret entrance to the laboratory. The cabinet door was open a crack.

I opened it all the way and went down the stairs into the lab. The bottom door was open as well. But the last time Tibert and I had been down here, he had closed and locked the door.

The Russians had been down here. And suddenly their actions became clear to me. By using American caliber weapons, and by killing their own people, they hoped to place the blame on the Americans. It would muddy up the investigation long enough for them to get the RVB-A delivery systems ready.

But there had to be witnesses, which also meant that they had allowed Lana, Tien Sing and Jean-Père to escape. But escape to where?

Back upstairs, I closed and locked the cabinet door and outside went across to my snowtrack where I pulled out the map Theisen had given me. I took it inside to the day room.

They were not here on the installation. At least I had not been able to find them. Nor were any of the remaining snowtracks missing from the garage. If they had left, and had not been carried off by the Soviets, then they had gone on foot.

I spread the map out on the table and searched the area around the installation.

About four miles out, to the east and in the opposite direction the Russians had gone, was a small mark with a weather station symbol. There was another about the same distance out to the south.

Two weather stations. Probably remotely controlled. But most certainly offering shelter for the maintenance crews who would have had to go out there from time to time.

But had Lana and the others known about them? And had they been able to make it four miles on foot?

Back down the corridor to where I had found Stalnov's body, I opened the door and stepped outside, switching on my flashlight.

There were footprints here in the snow. They led away from the building to the east.

I turned and looked back down the corridor. The fighting had begun in the day room and had caused the others to fall back here.

Lana, Tien Sing, and Jean-Père had probably left this way. Stalnov, not believing he too would be a victim, had come after them. But he had never made it. By the time he had gotten this far, they had come up behind him and fired.

Stepping back inside, I closed and latched the door, then went back through the building, once again out to my snowtrack where I got in and started the engine.

I drove slowly around the front of the building along the housing wing. At the back door I picked up the footprints in the twin beams from my headlights.

Driving over the top of them, I headed east, the same way they had gone.

Their tracks led up a gradual rise and at the top behind a gracefully sloping snowbank, they evidently stopped because the snow was trampled down in a tight area.

I got out of the machine and looked back down toward the installation. They had apparently stopped here and watched what was going on below, continuing only after they were convinced that their attackers meant to leave no one alive.

Back in the snowtrack, I continued to follow their tracks to the east.

Twice over the next couple of miles they had stopped to rest. At the second place there was a large depression in the snow, with footprints leading back to it. One of them had apparently fallen, and the others had come back to help.

About a mile farther on, the terrain began to rise, and a few hundred yards in the distance I was just able to pick out the small dome covering a weather radar unit.

I sped up, the big machine lumbering up the gentle slope toward the weather station, the three sets of footprints heading up as well.

At the top I stopped the machine, shut off the engine, and was about to climb out when a bullet whined off the hood a couple of inches in front of the windshield.

I dove to the right, over the passenger seat, as a second and third shot were fired from the weather station building, one of them crashing through the windshield where my head had just been.

Carefully I reached out, opened the passenger side door, and tumbled out into the snow as three more shots were fired in quick succession, slamming into the side of the snowtrack.

"Lana, it's me!" I shouted over the wind. "Stop firing!"

The shooting stopped.

"It's me, Nick Carter," I shouted from where I was crouched behind the snowtrack.

"Put your hands over your head and step out away from your machine," a man shouted from the weather station.

"Jean-Père, is it you?"

"Hands over your head now! Step out into plain view."

It was Jean-Père, or at least it sounded like him. Yet I had no way of knowing for sure if this was a ruse. "Is Dr. Edwards with you?" I called out.

A shot whined off the hood of the snowtrack, and a woman shouted.

"No . . . no! Nick, it's me!"

"Lana?"

"It's me, Nick."

"Are you all right?" I shouted.

"Yes. But they murdered the others . . . I . . . we thought you were a part of it."

"I'm coming out now," I shouted. "Hold your fire."

"Hands over your head!" Jean-Père said.

I raised my hands over my head, then got to my feet and stepped around the front of the machine. The beam from a flashlight was shined in my face, and a few seconds later Lana came across from behind the weather dome.

"Thank God it's you, Nick," she said, throwing herself into my arms.

Jean-Père, holding a rifle, appeared out of the darkness to my right; then Tien Sing, holding the flashlight appeared from the left.

"What happened back there?" I asked parting from Lana.

"You tell us, Captain Carter!" the Frenchman snapped.

"Everyone is dead," I said.

"We know, we watched it," Lana said.

"That's right," Jean-Père interjected. "We watched your people come in. At first we thought they had come to help us, but when they shut down the generator, we knew that was wrong."

I was shaking my head. "It wasn't the Americans,

Jean-Père, it was the Russians."

"Then why did they kill Stalnov?"

I looked beyond Jean-Père toward the weather station building. "Is there shelter here?"

"Answer me, Captain, or I will kill you here and now," the Frenchman shouted, starting to raise his rifle.

I stepped quickly to the left and easily grabbed the rifle from him, then jumped back.

"No!" Lana screamed.

"I didn't kill anyone, nor did the Americans," I shouted them down. "It was the Russians, and we've got to stop them before it's too late."

They all stared at me.

"Inside," I said. I clicked the rifle's safety back on and handed the weapon to Jean-Père. "Inside. I've got a lot to tell you. None of it very comforting."

Jean-Père looked from the rifle, back up to my face, and he finally nodded. "I'm sorry," he said.

"I understand. Have you any food here?"

"Plenty," Lana said, and the four of us trudged the rest of the way up the hill and went inside.

The weather station consisted of only three rooms; one that was unheated, which contained the weather radar antenna; one that housed the electronic weather monitoring equipment; and one that served as emergency living quarters in case the station maintenance people got stranded out here during a storm.

I took off my heavy mittens and parka, sat down at the long table, and lit myself a cigarette. Jean-Père and Tien Sing sat down across from me. Lana brought all of us coffee, then busied herself heating some soup for me.

"What makes you think your attackers were American?" I asked.

"They were wearing U.S. Navy uniforms, and their snowcats were marked with U.S. Naval insignia," Jean-Père said.

"Did you hear them talk?"

"No," Jean-Père said, and Tien Sing shook his head.

"They just came in and started shooting, Nick," Lana said from across the room. "It was terrible. I just couldn't believe it."

For just a moment I wondered if my own government had pulled some kind of a double-cross here to protect whatever had been going on in the secret laboratory beneath the generator building. But then I dismissed the thought. Stalnov was a KGB officer, and from what the Russians themselves had told me, something *was* definitely going on with them.

"They were Russian," I said at last.

"If that's so, then why did they kill Stalnov? He was one of theirs," Jean-Père asked.

For the third time then, I went through the story of all that had happened to me, and all that I had learned.

At first they were skeptical; I could see it in their eyes. But as I continued, their skepticism turned to incredulity and finally anger.

"At the Congress of Genetic Scientists last year in Geneva, we discussed this very possibility," Lana said bringing me my soup and a piece of bread and butter. "The Soviet delegation was the loudest in its criticism of that line of study."

"Understandably so," I said. "They knew they were close to a breakthrough down here, and they didn't want anyone else beating them to the punch."

She sat down across from me. "And now you say they've developed the material?"

"It's what killed the installation scientists. I suspect there was an accident not too far from the camp. Some of the material evidently escaped and killed our people."

"Then it's still out there?" Tien Sing asked.

"Presumably. But their sub will be off these shores in less than thirty-six hours to pick the material up."

"It has to be stopped, Nick. It has to be destroyed," Lana said.

"That's what I'm here for," I said. "But I'm going to need some information, and then some help."

"What have you got in mind?" Jean-Père asked.

I pushed the soup aside and sat forward. "How far could the RVB-A travel through the air in this climate?"

Lana shook her head. "There is no way of knowing that, Nick. Not without a sample of the material."

"Could we talk in terms of miles, or would it be yards or feet," I insisted. "What I'm trying to get at is a reasonable guess as to how far away the material was released when it killed our people."

"Certainly we could talk in terms of miles," Lana said. "Even down here. But beyond that . . ." she shrugged. "Five miles. Maybe ten at the outside."

"All right," I said. "Ten miles. Somewhere within a ten mile radius of the installation, probably to the west, the stuff is stockpiled, or just lying out there in the open for all we know. What is the stuff, a powder? A gas?"

"Probably gaseous. Stored in canisters."

"How can it be neutralized?" I asked.

Lana shook her head without hesitation. "It can't be. At least not yet."

"So we can't just destroy the stuff," I said half to myself. "We have to physically take it away from the Russians before they get it loaded aboard the submarine."

"Impossible," Jean-Père said softly.

"Seems that way, doesn't it?" I answered.

CHAPTER THIRTEEN

We made it back to the research installation a couple of hours later just before the full fury of the storm, which had arrived earlier than predicted, struck with its high winds, blowing snow, and even colder temperatures.

Within an hour we had cleaned up the mess, putting the four bodies in the pathology lab with the others.

While Lana and Dr. Tien Sing were in the lab going through Elsie de Hoorn's notes, looking for clues about the deadly RVB-A that might help us, Jean-Père and I went into the garage where we readied one of the two remaining snowtracks.

"I'm sending Lana back to the base at McMurdo," I explained.

"What about the Russians, *monsieur?* You said they had taken your base?"

"To look for me," I said. "But even if they're still there, it'll take her at least ten hours to make the trip. By then we will have made our move and the Soviets will know that I didn't go to New Zealand."

The Frenchman had been putting the radio direction finder from my snowtrack into the one Lana was going to use, and he stopped what he was doing and looked up at me.

"You still have not told us what you intend doing."

"That's because I didn't know myself until we got back here."

"And now?"

I had been refueling the machine, and I put the gas can down, wiped my hands on a rag, and came over to him.

"Lana tells me that the bio safe suits we brought with us may be effective against the RVB-A," I said.

Jean-Père shook his head. "She said *may* be. There is no way of knowing that for certain. Not unless there was something in Dr. de Hoorn's notes."

"Somewhere out there the Russians probably had an accident with the material. I think they were trying to transport it to the place where they were going to rendezvous with their sub when they had some kind of an accident. There was a crash, or something, but one of the tanks probably developed a leak."

"That's very possible, Captain Carter. I don't think they would have risked killing off the people here merely to experiment with the effectiveness of their material."

"So now they're out there picking up the canisters and bringing them to the rendezvous point."

"How will we stop them?"

"All we have to do is get close enough to the canisters, point a rifle at one of them, and threaten to blow it open unless they cooperate."

"Mon Dieu," the Frenchman said softly. "You would do that? You would kill all those soldiers?"

"You know what's at stake here," I said. "What would you do?"

"Radio the U.N. Tell the world what is happening."

"There's not enough time for that. Once that material is loaded aboard their nuclear sub, it will be too late. We have to stop them before then."

Jean-Père was having trouble dealing with what I was saying to him. He shook his head. "No, *monsieur*. I will not be a party to this insane plan of yours."

"Fine," I said. "You can return to McMurdo with Dr. Edwards. If need be I'll do it myself as soon as the storm lifts." I turned and headed for the door back into the living quarters.

"No," the Frenchman shouted. I turned around. He was holding a pistol on me.

"You will kill me, Dr. Jean-Père?"

"If need be."

"One more body for the pathology lab? Before long we'll have to make another room ready as a morgue. We're running out of space."

"I will not let you do this, Captain. We're all returning to McMurdo as soon as the storm lifts. There we will radio the United Nations Secretary General. It will be his decision."

"It will be too late," I snapped.

"There will be no more killing!"

"Are you working for the Russians then, is that it?"

"I have only your word that our people here were killed by the Soviets. They were wearing American uniforms and driving American vehicles. And you have admitted that your people were operating a secret genetic research laboratory here."

"To come up with the universal antidote for what the Soviet scientists were developing."

"Words . . . words. Nothing but words, Captain."

"And bodies in the pathology lab," I shouted. "Stacked like cordwood!"

Jean-Père's hand holding the pistol was shaking. "The killing has to stop!"

"If the Russians get that material back to the Soviet Union, Jean-Père, the killing will have just begun," I said. I turned once again, opened the door, and went back into the living quarters just as Lana Edwards was coming down the corridor from the pathology lab. She looked tired, and when she saw me she shook her head.

Together we went into the dining hall where we got ourselves a cup of coffee. Together we sat down at one of the tables.

"There's no way of making absolutely certain that the material won't penetrate our bio suits," she said.

I lit us both a cigarette. "We've got your machine ready. We'll all get some rest, and then you're returning to McMurdo. Jean-Père is going with you."

"Didn't you hear me?" she said, frustrated. "I don't know if you'll be safe in a bio suit."

"It doesn't matter," I said softly. "It has to be done. They have to be stopped."

"Christ," she said running her fingers through her hair. But then she looked up, a new expression on her face. "Did you say Jean-Père is coming back to McMurdo with me?"

I nodded. "He wants to radio the U.N. Secretary General. Lay it all in his lap."

"That sounds like the best idea I've heard so far."

"There isn't the time."

She sat forward, suddenly earnest. "What if you're wrong, Nick. What if something else is happening down here that none of us know about?"

"I can't afford to take the risk of doubting whether or not I'm right. If I am, and I don't do a thing about it, we could be at war within a month. A war, Lana, that we simply could not win at this moment."

For a long time then we held our silence, listening to the storm rage outside.

"Dr. Tien Sing will help you," Lana finally broke the silence. "He hates the Russians."

"No," I said. "I'm sending him back with you and Jean-Père."

She started to protest, but I held her off.

"You're all scientists, not soldiers. You'd just be in the way. I'll do this alone. Meanwhile, once you get back to McMurdo, you can do as Jean-Père wants. Radio the U.N. Tell them what's happening down here. If I don't make it, at least everyone will know what the Soviets are up to. It might help."

"I hope you're wrong, Nick," Lana said softly.

"So do I," I said. But I didn't think I was. I got up. "I'm going to get some sleep now. As soon as the storm lifts we'll leave."

Lana got to her feet. "I'm going back to the lab for a while to help Dr. Tien Sing. Maybe we can come up with something a little more conclusive for you."

Out in the corridor I ran into Jean-Père, but he refused to meet my eyes as he turned and hurried back down to the day room. Perhaps he was having second thoughts, and felt guilty about holding a gun on me.

I went back to the room I had used before, pulled off my boots and climbed gratefully into bed. I pulled the thick quilted covers over me and fell instantly to sleep.

I awoke with a start in the dark, silent room. Silence. There was no wind outside. The storm had passed.

Pushing the covers back, I got out of bed, quickly dressed in the dark, then went to the bathroom where I splashed some cold water on my face.

It was a little past four P.M. according to my watch, which meant I had slept ten hours. In less than twenty hours the Soviet nuclear submarine would be off the Antarctic coast near Mt. Sabine. I was a long way from there with a lot to do before I made it that far.

The others had evidently not gotten up yet, because

the lab, day room, and dining hall were deserted. I poured myself a cup of stale coffee, adding a generous shot of brandy to it from the bottle on the counter, and then went back into the housing wing where I knocked on Lana's door.

There was no answer, and after a moment I opened the door and looked inside. She wasn't there. Nor had her bed been slept in.

Suddenly I had the sinking feeling that I knew exactly what had happened while I had been sleeping. Quickly I checked Jean-Père's room, then Tien Sing's. Neither man was there, nor had their beds been slept in.

I tossed the coffee cup down and raced back to the garage. The main service doors were open, but only a small amount of snow had blown inside. The machine Jean-Père and I had made ready was gone. The hood on the only other machine here in the garage was open, the distributor cap from the engine lying beside it on the concrete floor. It was smashed into a hundred pieces.

In the day room, I pulled on my parka and went outside to the snowtrack I had brought up from McMurdo Sound. Its hood was open, the ignition wires ripped out, and the distributor cap smashed. All the supplies I had brought with me were missing.

Inside once again, I returned to the garage where I took a closer look at the damage Jean-Père had done to the small snowtrack vehicle. Besides the smashed distributor cap, he had ripped out the ignition coil wire. Other than that, however, there didn't seem to be anything wrong with the machine.

Within ten minutes I had found a spare distributor cap in one of the supply cabinets and had made up a new coil wire. Next, I filled the fuel tank from one of the drums outside, and finally started the engine to make sure it ran. It turned over immediately.

I let it warm up for a minute or two, then pulled it out

of the garage and around front next to the other machine.

The sky was clear, and there was no wind, but the
temperatures were bitterly cold, at least sixty below,
perhaps lower.

I left the snowtrack running while I went inside. I
found an M2 carbine and a couple of clips of ammunition among the supplies, some food, a survival tent, and
a large flashlight. It took me two trips to get all that
packed into the snowtrack, and on the third I went looking for the bio suits.

I found them on the floor in the pathology lab. Someone—probably Jean-Père—had taken a knife or a
scalpel to them, ripping the material to shreds. The suits
were useless now.

The man had wanted to stop me. He had done everything he could think of. I didn't believe he was a Soviet
agent. But he was dangerously naive. And although his
actions had not stopped me, they could very possibly
have cost me my life.

If need be, I still planned on putting a hole in one of
the RVB-A canisters, bio suit or not. No matter what
happened, the Soviets had to be stopped.

Zippering up my parka and pulling on my heavy mittens, I went back outside and climbed behind the
snowtrack's control column.

The tracks from the Soviet machines had been covered up in the storm, but they had led out to the west.
Five miles, maybe ten miles out. They would have been
pinned down by the storm, just as I had been, so there
was a very good chance they'd still be out there.

I put the machine in gear, swung it around so I was
heading west, and headed out and away from the research installation. For now it was the sole property of
the dead.

Within a couple of minutes I was far enough away so

that looking back I could no longer see the installation. A sudden sense of an almost overwhelming aloneness came over me. Washington, D.C., AXE, and David Hawk were on another planet, for as much good they could do me at this time and place.

I've always been a loner, and I've faced death literally hundreds of times. But for some reason, down here it was hard to keep track of just who you were, who you were fighting and why.

I was driving without headlights, the stars in the crystal clear sky providing plenty of illumination, making the ice hummocks and distant icy slopes seem like unreal, ghostly images.

After a while I turned down the instrument lights on the dash panel, to save my night vision as much as possible.

My thoughts turned even more morose. Even if I did manage to capture the deadly RVB-A canisters intact, what would become of them? Lana had told me that there was still no way of neutralizing the material—at least as far as she knew. Transporting the material back to the United States would be far too dangerous. If the canisters developed a leak, it would mean disaster.

They would have to remain here, on Antarctica, where even if and when they did develop leaks, the danger would be minimized because of the relative lack of population and the exceedingly harsh climate.

I had been driving for what seemed like hours, but probably wasn't much more than thirty minutes or so, when I saw a flash of light ahead. I slammed on the brakes, and when I had the snowtrack stopped, I shut off the engine, climbed out, and shoved my parka hood back.

Almost immediately I could hear the sounds of several engines, of metal clanking against metal, of people talking and shouting.

It was hard to tell just how far away they were because of the way sounds carried in the ultra-cold air. But they were not far. Half a mile perhaps.

I flipped my parka hood back up, went back to the snowtrack, and from inside grabbed the flashlight and the M2 carbine, which I loaded with one of the thirty-round clips, pocketing the other.

Then I headed toward the source of the sounds, stopping every few yards to make sure I was moving in the right direction.

A quarter of a mile away the terrain sloped upwards, and at the top I suddenly saw dozens of lights from as many snowtrack machines. I could also see twenty or thirty men, a portable generator, and a string of strong lights on tripods illuminating a wide crack in the ice.

As I watched, something was winched up from the crevasse, and two men, working with what was obviously extreme caution, carried it to a large cargo sled attached to one of the larger snowtrack vehicles.

I understood immediately what had happened, and what they were doing down there.

Someone had been transporting the canisters of RVB-A to the coastal rendezvous point with the submarine when the vehicle they were driving plunged down into the crevasse. One or more of the canisters had broken open, killing the driver, and eventually killing the scientists at our own research installation.

The only explanation that I could think of for the transport driver to have come this close to the American installation was that he had gotten lost.

Now the Soviets had found the canisters and were loading them aboard another transport, and in eighteen or nineteen hours would meet the submarine. Unless I could stop them.

I backed off so that the crest of the hill was between me and the Soviet work party. I then circled far to the right before I once again pushed through the snow to the top.

I was at least a quarter of a mile above and to the right of them. I was banking on the fact that their night vision would be ruined from working under the lights and their attention diverted by their work.

Crouching low, I started down the hill directly in line with a couple of their snowtracks, keeping my eyes on the nearest of the troops.

There was no way possible that they would be able to hear my approach over the sounds of the generator supplying the electricity for the lights; nevertheless, I moved slowly, each step careful and deliberate.

About fifty yards from the nearest vehicle, one of the armed men turned in my direction, and I froze where I was.

For several long, horrible seconds the man stared directly at me. He must have been able to see something, yet his night vision was so blurred by the lights he apparently thought he was seeing nothing more than an ice hummock, or a shadow, because he turned away.

I waited a little while longer, then on my hands and knees crawled to the right, putting the nearest snowtrack between me and the soldier.

When I finally reached the concealment of the machine, I stood up, then edged around to the front of it.

I was only thirty feet from the crevasse, but still on the opposite side of the work party from where the canisters were being loaded on the transport sled fifty yards away.

It would be impossible to cross that distance without being discovered and cut down. Impossible, that is, dressed the way I was, in a U.S. Navy parka.

I unzipped the front of my heavy mittens, reached inside my parka, and pulled out my stiletto. The intense cold numbed my fingers even through the mitten's silk inner glove, so I was going to have to be quick about this.

Working my way back around the snowtrack, I was less than fifteen feet away from the soldier who had stared out at me. The next nearest man was twenty yards or more away, near the first lights.

I opened the back of the snowtrack, and the soldier spun around at the slight noise, bringing his rifle up.

"Over here," I said in Russian. "Be quick about it!"

The man hesitated a moment. He could see me through the side windows of the snowtrack, but I didn't think he could tell what kind of parka I was wearing.

I pulled a crate out of the back. "Move it!" I snapped. "We don't have all night!"

The soldier finally slung his rifle over his shoulder and trudged back to where I was waiting for him.

As he stepped around the back of the snowtrack, I reached out with my left hand, grabbed his parka, and pulled him all the way around and out of sight of the work party. Then I brought the stiletto up to his throat.

"Make a noise and you die instantly, comrade," I hissed.

The man's eyes went wide, and he tried to struggle out of my grasp, pulling me forward; momentarily off balance, my blade buried itself in his throat.

He coughed once, blood spurting from the wound, as he jerked violently to the left, opening a much larger wound in his neck.

I pulled him back down behind the snowtrack as his struggling became weaker and weaker, and finally his body went limp in my arms, and I eased him down to the snow.

"Damn," I swore to myself. I hadn't wanted to kill him. I quickly checked to make sure that no one had noticed what had happened back here, then unzippered the soldier's parka and pulled it off his body.

He was a young boy. Probably no more than twenty-two or twenty-three, and it made me angry that he had to die this way. So much killing, senseless killing. And yet I had to keep thinking about the canisters they were pulling out of the crevasse. If I didn't stop their shipment back to the Soviet Union, it was very possible that millions would die.

I took my parka off and pulled on the soldier's, then replaced my stiletto in its sheath and grabbed the young man's Kalashnikov rifle.

Making sure the fur-lined hood was drawn tightly around my face, I stepped out away from the snowtrack and moved back to where the young soldier had been standing before he had come back at my call.

Fifty yards away two men were starting to pull a canvas cover over the back of the transport sled that was now stacked with small canisters. At the crevasse, several men were beginning to dismantle the winch, and others were beginning to shut down the lights, one by one.

They had finished. I was going to have to move immediately!

Flipping the Kalashnikov's safety off, I headed purposefully toward the transport sled.

For the first ten yards no one noticed me, but then someone to my right shouted something that I couldn't quite catch, and I continued.

"Sergeant," someone else shouted.

When I was halfway there, two men broke away from a group by one of the snowtracks and headed toward me in a dead run, their weapons coming up.

I swiveled, fired a short burst at them, then broke to the right at an angle that would put me between the crevasse and the loaded snowtrack sled.

Half a dozen men suddenly appeared between me and

the sled, and I had to dodge farther right as they brought their weapons up and opened fire.

Something slammed into my left side, causing me to lose my balance. I slipped and fell to my knee.

Blood was pounding in my ears as I started to bring my weapon around, but at that moment the ice and snow beneath me suddenly gave way, and I was falling, the edge of the crevasse crumbling away.

CHAPTER FOURTEEN

When I came to moments later, I was half buried in the snow, where I lay wedged between the wall of the crevasse and something hard. Far above me, I could see the reflection of lights, and hear the sounds of the Russian snowtracks starting up and pulling away.

My side hurt where I had been shot. But the heavy parka had evidently deflected the bullet so that it just grazed my ribs.

I was beginning to struggle out of the deep snow when a strong light was shined on me from above, and I lay still. If they thought I was still alive down here, they'd probably finish the job.

The cold seeped into me as the lights continued to search the bottom of the crevasse where I lay, but then someone above shouted something, the light went out, and a minute or two later the last of the snowtracks left, leaving me in absolute silence.

I waited a full five minutes longer to make sure that they had not left someone behind to watch for me. But gradually I began to understand that it didn't matter to them if I was alive or dead. The lip of the crevasse was at least fifty feet above me. There was no way for me to get out of there. At least not at this spot.

Finally I pushed my way up out of the snow, pulled my flashlight out, and turned it on. I was standing between the wall of the crevasse and a wrecked snowtrack machine. Lying on its side, above and to the left of the vehicle was a transport sled.

This evidently was the machine that had been used to transport the RVB-A canisters to the submarine rendezvous. I had been correct in my guess. For some reason the driver had become lost, and had driven his machine into this crevasse.

Shoveling the snow with my hands, I cleared the door on the passenger side, and, although the machine's frame was badly bent, managed to pull the door open and shine my flashlight beam inside.

A man in a Soviet uniform lay back against the driver's side door. His eyes were open, and his tongue, which he had bitten completely through, protruded from his mouth. There was a great deal of frozen blood down the front of his parka.

He looked the same as the scientists at our research installation. One of the RVB-A canisters had evidently sprung a leak in the crash, and he had been the first one to die from the agent.

I climbed into the cab of the snowtrack, then crawled over the seats to the rear of the machine. There was a pack that contained food, a first-aid kit, a fire extinguisher, and a kit containing tools and spare parts for the snowtrack. But there was no rope, no chains, no climbing gear of any kind.

I pulled out a couple of the ration packs, stuffed them in my coat pockets, then crawled back into the front of the machine.

It was becoming increasingly hard to move—or even to think straight—in the intense cold that was numbing my entire body.

For a long time I was content just to sit there in the snowtrack and stare out the shattered windshield at the walls of the crevasse. Comfortable where I was. No reason to move. No reason to do anything. . . .

Finally, however, I shook myself out of the lethargy that had come over me enough to understand that if I remained here doing nothing I would die. I would freeze to death, and there would be no one to stop the Soviets from rendezvousing with their submarine.

I struggled out the door of the snowtrack, climbed up on the hood, then jumped down to the floor of the crevasse.

The crack in the ice was at least fifty feet deep, the walls about fifteen feet apart down here, but about forty or fifty feet apart at the top, and too steep for me to climb.

I started forward, my boots crunching on the loose snow. There was a possibility that further along the crevasse the floor would rise up to the top, or the walls would slope away so that I could climb out.

About a hundred feet away from the wrecked snowtrack, I was sure I heard a noise from above, and I stopped, pulled my parka hood back, and listened.

For a few seconds I couldn't hear a thing, but then it came again. It was a snowtrack. I recognized the sound. The Russians were coming back, probably to make sure I was really dead.

I flipped off my flashlight and raced back to the wrecked vehicle as the machine above came closer and closer. A light flashed overhead as I jumped up on the hood, scrambled over the side and crawled inside the machine.

I pulled my Luger out, levered a round into the chamber, and clicked the safety off. From above they would not be able to see me sitting here in the machine.

They would have to send someone down.

The snowtrack was directly above me now, its engine idling.

A light shined down searching the crevasse floor and finally centered on the wrecked vehicle. I tensed.

"Nick!" a woman's voice came from above. "Nick," she screamed again. "Can you hear me?" It was Lana!

I climbed out the door and up on the hood. "Lana? Is that you?" I shouted up.

The beam of a flashlight caught me in the eyes. "Nick . . . oh God, Nick, you're alive," Lana shouted.

"And cold," I shouted. "Have you got a rope?"

"Yes," she said. "Just a moment."

"Are you all right, Captain?" Jean-Père called down. He had come back.

"I'm okay. How did you know I was down here?"

"We watched the entire thing," he said. "Wait a minute."

The light was gone, plunging me into darkness for just a second, then it was back.

"I'm going to throw down a rope. Tie it around your chest. I'll hook the other end to the snowtrack and we'll pull you up."

"Go ahead," I shouted. I clicked the safety on and stuffed the Luger in my pocket. A second later the rope came down. I jumped off the hood and grabbed the end, looping it around my chest and tying it off.

"Ready down here," I shouted up.

"Hold on," Jean-Père shouted.

The snowtrack's engine revved up, and the slack came up on the rope, nearly pulling me off my feet.

"Here we go," Jean-Père shouted, and I was being pulled slowly upwards, using my feet to keep away from the uneven surface of the crevasse wall.

Then I was up on the surface, snow and large chunks

of ice cascading back down into the crevasse.

Jean-Père and Tien Sing helped me to my feet, untied the rope, and then helped me back to the snowtrack where I climbed in the passenger side, the sudden warmth almost overpowering.

Jean-Père got in on the driver's side, and Tien Sing and Lana climbed in the rear, tossing the coil of rope in the back.

For several minutes we sat in silence, the only sounds the snowtrack's idling engine and the heater fan pouring out its warmth.

"Why did you come back?" I finally asked.

Jean-Père looked away. "Dr. Edwards convinced me," he said softly.

"Convinced you of what?"

He looked at me. "To come back and get you. Nothing more. Although . . . although I was wrong. I see it now."

"We weren't gone more than a couple of hours," Lana said from the back. "When we got back to the installation you were gone."

"So you followed my tracks out here?"

"I forgot about the spare parts cabinet," Jean-Père said sheepishly. "Do you want to go back up the hill for your snowtrack?"

I glanced over my shoulder toward the back of the machine. "Did you bring the weapons?"

"They're back there," Jean-Père said. Tien Sing was grinning.

"Then we don't need the other machine," I said.

"What next?"

"We follow them and stop them before they load the canisters aboard the sub."

"I counted at least fifty men," Jean-Père said.

"The odds aren't the best, but once they stop at the

coast and the darkness comes, they'll be vulnerable. All
we have to do is hold them off for ten hours until our
own sub arrives."

"Is that all," Jean-Père said dryly.

"We can get the other machine," I snapped. "You can
take it back to McMurdo."

The Frenchman said nothing as he put the snowtrack
in gear and headed away from the crevasse along the line
the Russians had gone.

"Turn out the headlights," I said after we had gone a
mile or so. Jean-Père complied, and we continued, the
trail left by the dozen or more Soviet vehicles easy to
follow in the light from the clear night sky.

A couple of hours later we still had not made contact
with the Soviet column, and Jean-Père stopped our
snowtrack so that we could get out, stretch our legs, and
have something to eat.

While we were stopped I checked the rifles I had been
supplied with back at McMurdo Sound, loaded them,
and made sure all the ejector slides worked smoothly in
the low temperatures.

I also checked the radios. There was nothing on any
of the American channels, except for the radio direction
finder station, which broadcast its steady beam for one
hundred miles in every direction from the station.

Either the Russians were still in control of the American base on the Sound, or they had destroyed our radio
equipment, and our technicians had not been able to fix
it yet. Either way, we were on our own out here.

A couple of hours later we stopped again, and Jean-
Père crawled in the back and went to sleep as Lana
came up front with me. I drove.

For a long time then, we continued in silence, the
snowtrack bucking and heaving over the uneven terrain.

I continually searched the darkness ahead of us for any sign that we were coming up on the Russian column, or for a sign that they had left someone behind to act as a rear guard. But there was nothing—except the bleak, forbidding plain.

"What happens afterwards?" Lana asked, finally breaking the silence.

I glanced at her. "What do you mean?"

"I mean if we're successful. If we actually stop them from delivering the canisters. What then?"

"Then I've done my job."

"You know what I mean, Nick. What's going to happen to the bio agent?"

"I don't know, for sure. But it'll have to remain here on Antarctica. The stuff is too dangerous to move."

"Our government won't use it?"

I shook my head. "I don't think so, Lana. But it's up to you scientists to come up with a way of destroying it."

She thought about that for a moment. "From what you told us, Commander Tibert believed his people were on the verge of developing an antidote for the material."

"That's what he said."

"Then we should bring the canisters back to the research installation and keep them there until the antidote is developed. We can use it to destroy the RVB-A."

"Will you work on it?"

She shook her head. "Not down here. I'm going to return to California. I can be more effective there, in my own lab."

"We'll make it," I said softly. "We'll stop them."

"Sure," she said, but it was obvious she didn't believe me.

We stopped twice more over the next six hours or so, once for Lana to drive while I got some sleep, and once for Tien Sing to take the controls.

By three A.M., we had all managed to get some rest and something to eat. Two hours earlier we had sighted Mt. Sabine rising in the distance. The tracks from the Russian column curved to the north, directly toward the coast, and we had continued to follow them, but much more cautiously now that we were close.

The Soviet submarine was not due to rendezvous for another six hours yet, but I wanted to be in position as soon as possible, in case the sub arrived earlier than expected. If they actually managed to load the canisters aboard the sub, it would be too late for us to do anything about it.

I was driving again when the snowtrack's crevasse detector pinged its warning, and I stopped.

Ahead of us, in the still night, we could easily see the Russian column's tracks leading straight through the crevasse area, and then they disappeared over a hill about a half a mile away.

"We must be very close to the coast," Jean-Père said.

"It's right over that hill out there," I said studying the map in the dim overhead light. Just before the ice cap sloped down to the ocean, there was a narrow area of crevasses. We had reached that point now.

I refolded the map, put it aside, eased the snowtrack in gear, and drove slowly along the Russian tracks across the crevasse region, pulling up again just before the crest of the hill.

Zipping up my parka I looked at the others. "I'm going to the top of the hill on foot, to take a look. I want you all to stay here."

They all nodded their silent agreement, and I climbed out of the snowtrack, flipped up my hood, and trudged the rest of the way up the hill. The cold was unbelievably intense. Much worse than it had been before. I realized that, even dressed in cold weather gear, we would not be able to remain outside for much more than an hour at a stretch. It was going to make this job much more difficult, and yet we had no other choice. It had come down to us, here and now.

I hunched down the last few feet so that when I topped the rise I would not be silhouetted against the night sky. I didn't know whether or not they would post lookouts, but I suspected they would.

Just as I reached the top of the hill, a flash of light from below lit up the night sky, and a second or two later the sound of a large explosion rumbled up the hill.

I was in time to see a spume of ice and water rising high up into the sky, about a thousand feet below me, and at least a hundred yards away from the cluster of small buildings, around which were parked the Soviet snowtrack machines.

It took several minutes for the water and ice to settle enough so that I could see what had happened. There was now a huge hole in the ice, through which at least the submarine's conning tower could rise. They would load the canisters aboard the boat through one of the side hatches.

Several figures were moving down there across the ice from where they had hidden behind a snowtrack during the explosion. They approached the hole in the ice, did something there for several minutes, then retreated back to their machine, which they drove back to the buildings.

There was something on the ice near the large hole, and for a moment I thought they might have set another explosive charge to widen the hole even more. But then I suddenly understood that the equipment down there was probably some kind of a homing device for the sub to find the opening.

There was no other movement below, then, and as far as I could tell they had not posted any guards. Of course they could not suspect that anyone had followed them, yet it was a sloppy setup, especially considering the nature of the cargo they were carrying.

I eased back away from the crest, then stood up and hurried back to the snowtrack where the others were waiting for me.

"Are they down there?" Jean-Père asked when I climbed in behind the control column.

"They're down there all right," I said. I opened the map.

"What was the explosion?" Lana asked.

"They blew a hole in the ice so that their submarine could surface," I said without looking up. About five miles farther up the coast, there seemed to be another path down to the ocean level. From there, I was sure that we could get very close to the Soviet encampment without being detected.

I put the map aside, eased the snowtrack into gear, and headed back up the coast, driving parallel to the hilltop, but well below the crest.

"Where are we going, Captain Carter?" Tien Sing asked. "I thought we came here to kill Russians."

"We're here to stop the transfer of the canisters," I said.

"How?" Jean-Père asked.

"I'll show you in about fifteen minutes," I said, concentrating on my driving.

The hill began to flatten out in a couple of miles, and a few miles further it sloped naturally down to meet the level of the frozen ocean. I drove out to the edge of the icepack, then started back toward the Soviet rendezvous point.

Tien Sing pulled one of the rifles from the back of the

snowtrack and loaded it.

"There will be no firing until I give the signal," I said sharply.

"They've killed a lot of good people," Tien Sing said.

"There are fifty of them, heavily armed. If we go in there blasting away we wouldn't have a chance. We're going to do this my way. Understood?"

There was a silence in the cab for a long moment.

"He's right," Lana said gently.

Tien Sing finally nodded. "What is it you are going to do, Captain?"

In many spots along the icepack, pressure ridges had formed in the ice, pushing huge blocks up in a jumble of fantastic angles. I stopped behind one of the piles and flipped on the interior lights.

"The Soviet sub is going to be here within the next five hours, but our submarine won't be arriving until at least seven tonight. That's a long time from now. Too long a time for us to have any hope of holding off fifty men."

"Then we must kill them," Tien Sing said.

"We don't have the firepower. If just a few of them made it to their snowtracks they could easily come up behind us. We wouldn't have a chance."

"So what are you proposing, Captain?" Jean-Père asked.

I grinned. "I'm going to sneak in there and pull the distributor caps off all their machines."

Tien Sing laughed out loud. "All except one, Captain Carter," he said. "All but the one attached to the cargo sled."

"That's right. If they're on foot, and we steal the canisters, they won't be able to do too much about it."

"What if they have guards posted?" Lana asked.

"I didn't see any."

"But if they do?" she insisted.

I looked away. "I'll have to kill them."

"I'm going with you," Tien Sing said.

"So will I," Jean-Père said. "It would take too long for one or two men to work on all the machines." He smiled. "Besides, I've become something of an expert at it."

"Good," I said, and I turned to Lana. "You'll stay with the machine. If anything goes wrong, I want you to head back to McMurdo Sound. Tell them what happened."

"I'm frightened, Nick," she said.

"Everyone is," I said.

I checked my Luger, then put the snowtrack in gear and continued up the coast, stopping every few hundred yards to get out and stand on the roof to look ahead.

The temperature outside had to be approaching the eighty below zero mark, and even the powerful heater in the snowtrack was having trouble keeping the ice off the inside of the windshield.

A few minutes later I stopped again at the edge of another pressure ridge, and when I climbed up to look I could see the Russian encampment, a dozen or so snowtrack machines parked around the buildings.

"We go on foot from here," I said climbing back inside.

"How far is it?" Jean-Père asked.

"A quarter of a mile. And it looks quiet. No lights. They're probably sleeping."

"Be careful, Nick," Lana said.

"We will. But if anything goes wrong I want to know that you'll be heading back to McMurdo."

She nodded.

I looked at the others. "Ready?"

They nodded, and we got out of the snowtrack and

headed as fast as we could move through the snow, down the coast toward the Soviet rendezvous point.

CHAPTER FIFTEEN

It took us about ten minutes to reach the first row of Russian snowtracks. We hunched down behind them, breathing shallowly. Over-exertion in these temperatures would result in painful frosted lungs.

We could hear music coming from one of the buildings, probably from a tape recorder or portable record player, and several men singing. They definitely were not expecting trouble here.

After a few moments I moved to the front of the machine, unlatched the hood, and eased it open. There was enough light from the moon for me to just make out the distributor cap, and I reached inside and pulled out all the ignition wires, then unclipped the cap and pulled it out.

Jean-Père and Tien Sing were watching me. I looked up, smiled, then dropped the distributor cap on the ice and crushed it with my boot heel.

We had counted fourteen machines, plus the one attached to the cargo sled. One down, thirteen to go, I thought as I softly closed the hood.

I motioned for Jean-Père to take the machines to the right and Tien Sing the machines parked to the left of the buildings.

They headed off silently into the night as I moved to the second machine in this group, opened its hood, ripped out the ignition wires, and pulled out and destroyed the distributor cap.

We worked as quickly as we could, but in the intense cold it was very difficult to move fast. After a half hour of work, we had done all but two machines, which were parked near the snowtrack attached to the cargo sled.

I had just finished with the last machine in my group and was closing the hood as Jean-Père and Tien Sing were making their way across to the cargo sled. I was about to step around the machine and join them when the music from one of the buildings suddenly got louder, and a splash of yellow light fell across the snow.

Someone shouted something, and the light disappeared. A man dressed in cold weather gear stood in front of the building, looking directly my way. The cargo sled and the other machines were between him and Jean-Père and Tien Sing, but I could see them both. They had not heard the music or seen the light, and they were continuing across to the machines.

If they unlatched the hoods and opened them, the Russian by the door would definitely hear them and sound the alarm.

Quickly I moved around to the back of the snowtrack I was hiding behind as I pulled my stiletto from its sheath.

The man by the door was still standing there. But what the hell was he doing outside in this kind of weather? Unless he had heard something and come out to investigate.

I was about thirty yards from him, too far a distance to throw the stiletto.

He stepped away from the building and turned to look toward the cargo sled. He stiffened and slowly brought his rifle up, then started slowly toward the laden sled.

Keeping low, I stepped around the back of the truck and headed as fast as I could toward the Russian. Anyone looking out the windows of the buildings, or stepping outside, would see me, and I wouldn't have a chance.

I was about fifteen yards behind the man when Jean-Père and Tien Sing evidently reached the snowtracks, because the hood on one of the machines came up.

"Who's there?" the man shouted in Russian.

In half a dozen steps I was on him as he was raising his rifle to his shoulder. With my left hand I grabbed him by the face, yanked his head back, and drove the stiletto through his thick parka into his chest.

It was a bad thrust, because he cried out and tried to struggle away from me. I buried the stiletto in his chest again ripping it viciously to the left, then the right.

The Russian shuddered and finally went limp in my arms. I let him drop to the snow and raced to where Jean-Père and Tien Sing were crouched behind the last two snowtracks.

"Do it," I shouted urgently.

Jean-Père jumped up and began pulling wires out of the snowtrack as I raced over to the cargo sled. Tien Sing evidently had pulled the distributor cap out of the other machine because he had his rifle up and at the ready.

At that moment, however, a deep, booming horn shattered the silence of the night, and we all spun around in time to see the conning tower of a submarine come fully out of the water, the hammer and sickle emblem clearly visible.

Tien Sing leaped out from around the snowtrack he had been hiding behind and opened fire as the door of

the nearest building burst open and several men came
out.

Two of them fell; the others pulled back and a second
later opened fire, cutting the Chinese doctor down.

Jean-Père stepped back from the open hood of the
snowtrack he had been working on, raised his rifle, and
fired into the engine compartment. Then he swung
around to the right and began firing toward the buildings.

He was hit at least a dozen times as I raced the opposite way around the cargo sled and slipped behind the
nearest building. Then the shooting died down. The
submarine's horn sounded again, the noise booming and
reverberating from the icepack a hundred yards away.

With my Luger out and the safety off, I raced to the
far end of the small building and peered around the corner.

The submarine's horn blasted again, echoing and re-
echoing off the ice hills behind the encampment. There
was a great deal of activity out front, but evidently I had
not been spotted, nor was my presence suspected, because there was no search going on. Instead their efforts
were being directed toward starting the cargo sled snowtrack.

Armed with nothing more than a Luger, a stiletto,
and a very small gas bomb, there was very little I could
do against such a well-armed force here and a submarine
crew a hundred yards away.

I ducked back around the building and leaned up
against the wall as I tried to think this out.

If Lana had done exactly what I had told her to do,
she would, at this moment, be on her way back to
McMurdo Sound. She would have heard the firing and
would have understood that something had gone wrong.

I looked around the corner of the building again.
They were evidently having some trouble starting the

cargo sled snowtrack, because they were beginning to unload the canisters and hand carry them down to the submarine.

I could see several heavily clad men on the deck of the sub. It would not take them very long, however, even by hand, to load all the canisters. And once the agent was aboard the sub and out to sea, it would be too late—far too late—to do anything about it.

There was only one thing left for me to do. Lana was gone; there were no usable vehicles here, and if I remained outside, I would freeze to death, so it didn't really matter.

I raced across to the next building, waited there a moment to see if I had been spotted, and then hurried along the rear of the last two buildings. Then I headed away from the encampment, moving as fast as I could, and keeping the buildings between me and the Russians.

I didn't think anyone would spot me. They had turned on their portable lighting units, and their attention would be directed to the job at hand.

Another five minutes and we would have made it, I thought bitterly as I ran, the freezing cold biting at my lungs, my heart hammering in my chest.

About five hundred yards out I began angling parallel to the ice pack and then began slowly circling back toward the pressure ridge behind which we had left Lana and the snowtrack.

I didn't think she would still be there, but I wanted to make sure. And it would be just as good a place as any other for me to do what I planned on doing.

It took me nearly twenty minutes to make it back to the pressure ridge. And in the dim starlight I could see where Lana had turned the snowtrack around and had headed back up the coast to where she could drive up on the plateau.

She was gone, and for several minutes I stayed there

trying to catch my breath. But I was running out of time. I had a long way to go yet.

I headed straight out onto the icepack, picking my way as best I could through the tangled, jumbled ice jungle of the pressure ridge area.

Twice I almost fell into deep cracks in the ice that led down into the open sea ten feet below, but both times I somehow managed to catch myself.

Finally I made it through the pressure region and immediately headed back toward the submarine. Only this time I would be approaching it from the sea side. I was going to have to be very careful that I wouldn't be spotted moving across the ice.

The snow was deep and heavily drifted out here, but almost immediately I spotted the lights back at the Soviet rendezvous point and the submarine's black sail jutting up out of the ice like some huge, ominous gravestone.

I circled wide, keeping low and behind as many snowdrifts as I could, finally coming to a spot a quarter of a mile out on the icepack, directly in line with the submarine and the Soviet encampment. Then I started back toward the shore.

If there was a lookout on the conning tower, or someone on the deck of the sub who happened to look my way, they could not help but spot me as a dark moving object against the white background.

As I ran across the ice, though, I could see only the sub, and beyond it, the lights from the Russian troops who were hand-loading the canisters aboard.

At a hundred yards out, I stopped to catch my breath before I continued. I moved more cautiously now that I was this close.

At fifty yards, someone came out of a hatch low in the side of the sail, and I dropped to my knees and froze where I was.

The man looked over the edge of the boat, down into the water, walked toward the back, then the front, then went back to the open hatch where he shouted something.

A couple of seconds later water bubbled and splashed up from the hole in the ice. The water had probably begun to refreeze and they had released compressed air from their ballast tanks to keep it clear, which could only mean that they were nearly ready to submerge.

An eternity later, the man seemed to be satisfied and he crawled back through the hatch and closed it behind him.

I jumped up and raced as fast as I could to the opening in the ice as the worklights back on shore began going out, one by one.

They were finished! The sub would be submerging at any moment.

The deck of the sub was about five feet across open water from the edge of the blasted-away hole in the ice. Without hesitation I jumped across, nearly slipping, and then hurried to the forward edge of the sail.

About thirty yards away, half a dozen stragglers were trudging back to the buildings, the last of the lights they had set up finally winking out.

The canisters were aboard. They had done their job.

About ninety feet forward was the emergency escape hatch. I looked toward it and then back at the departing troops. But they had stopped and turned around. They were watching the sub and waiting for it to submerge.

There wasn't a chance in hell of me making it all the way forward to the hatch, spinning it open, and then getting below without being spotted and shot at. Not a chance.

The submarine's engines started, the vibration coming up through the soles of my boots. The boat seemed to shudder, air bubbles making the water around us boil, and we began to submerge, the decks coming awash almost immediately.

Sea water was up to my knees by the time I managed to scramble back to the ladder that ran up the side of the sail to the bridge, and clamber up.

We were going down fast by the time I made it to the top, yanked out my Luger, flipped the safety off, and spun the hatch wheel.

When I pulled it open, an alarm Klaxon sounded from below, and a face appeared in the conning tower hatch.

I fired, the man's face erupting in a mass of blood, and then I was below, pulling the hatch closed overhead, and spinning the locking mechanism as we continued to submerge.

Several men were shouting orders below on the control-room deck as I fell the last few feet down the ladder and crawled to the lower hatch near where the crewman had fallen.

The captain and several of his officers were looking up as I appeared in the opening, my pistol raised.

"Your captain is a dead man!" I screamed in Russian.

A seaman appeared from the aft companionway, a rifle in his hand, and he started to raise it at the same moment I brought my Luger around and fired, catching him directly in the chest.

He was thrown back through the hatch, and again I brought my weapon to bear on the submarine commander.

"I'll kill him unless you do exactly as I say," I shouted.

They all slowly raised their hands. Everyone was looking up at me, except for the helmsman who was nervously running the ship.

"You have us for the moment. What do you want?" the captain said smoothly.

"I want everyone out of here except for you, the helmsman, and the radio operator. Then I want all the hatches aboard this vessel sealed. Immediately!"

"And if I do not comply?"

"I will shoot you, and all of your officers," I said, somewhat more in control now that I had caught my breath. "And believe me, Captain, I am capable of it."

"We would all die in that case," the man said. "Including you."

"Indeed," I said. "Three seconds! Three! Two! One!" I started to squeeze the trigger.

"Wait!" the captain shouted.

I eased up.

"Do as he says," the man snapped.

"But, Captain—" one of his officers began to protest.

"That is an order, Mr. Ryabov!"

"Aye aye, sir," the officer said.

One by one the others complied. When they were all gone except for the captain, one other officer, and the helmsman who had never left his position, the doors throughout the boat were sealed.

"Now that you have us, what do you want?" the captain asked.

"What's our status at this moment," I snapped.

Both the captain and the other officer looked toward the control panels above the helm. At that moment, their attention diverted, I swung around and scrambled down the ladder.

The captain smiled. "Well done," he said. "I wonder, however, how long you will be able to keep us at bay. You look as if you could use a hot meal and a good night's sleep."

"Long enough for us to reach the American installation at McMurdo Sound."

The captain's eyebrows rose.

"Your radio officer will immediately radio our base

with your intentions, and you will navigate and give the appropriate orders for us to arrive there within two hours. In two hours and one minute, if we haven't arrived, I will kill you and your radio officer and then call for your first officer and first engineer. Clear?"

The captain's eyes had narrowed, a faint flush in his cheeks. But he nodded. "You know what is aboard this vessel?"

I nodded.

"Then you know why it must be returned to my country as soon as humanly possible. I appeal to you—"

"Wait a minute, Captain," I said. "I know what is contained in those canisters that were loaded aboard. Do you?"

He started toward me, and I raised the Luger a little higher. "Don't make me kill you," I said tiredly. "It would be a waste."

He stopped.

"The canisters contain an extremely potent biological warfare agent."

"It is a lie."

"It is the truth, Captain. Twenty-nine of my people were killed by it when an accident occurred while your scientists were transporting it to your rendezvous point. An international commission was appointed to find out what happened. They were murdered by your people."

"The canisters contain the antidote for *your* bio agent."

I shook my head. "No. Divert to our base at McMurdo and it will be proven to you. As a matter of fact, the canisters can be left aboard until it's proven to your satisfaction."

The captain said nothing.

I was tired, yet I felt that I knew this man. He was a naval officer, nothing more. And I was sure that he honestly believed the story he had been told.

"I was sent down here to find out what happened," I said. "I did." I lowered my Luger, flipped the safety on, and stuffed it in my pocket.

The navigation officer started toward me, but the captain held him back.

"No!" he snapped. He looked at me for a long time. "It will be as you say for now."

I looked around the control room, then went across and sat down. "I would suggest, Captain, that you seal off the compartment where the canisters were loaded. A small leak in one of them could kill us all."

The captain seemed suddenly uncomfortable. "Part of my orders were to transport the material in a sealed compartment."

"Fine," I said, taking a deep breath and letting it out slowly. "Fine."

The U.S. nuclear attack submarine *Tyrannosaurus* lay side by side with the Soviet nuclear submarine *Solotkin,* locked until spring in the Antarctic icepack just off shore from the American base at McMurdo Sound.

A Soviet housekeeping delegation had been sent over to maintain the ice-locked sub, and its American counterpart was on duty aboard the *Tyrannosaurus.*

At diplomatic levels, absolutely no mention had been made, nor would it ever be made, of the canisters containing the RVB-A. In return, no mention was being made of the deaths that had occurred because of the Soviet research into biological warfare agents on Antarctica.

"A Mexican standoff," Hawk had called it when communications had been re-established.

"Unbelievable," Lana had fumed.

But it had been just one more play in a continuing

game in which the rules always changed, but in which the stakes always remained the same—world domination. This time we had nearly lost. And although frightening to think about, there would be a next time.

**DON'T MISS THE NEXT NEW
NICK CARTER SPY THRILLER**

APPOINTMENT IN HAIPHONG

Although we had been lucky so far and had not run into any patrols, Father Lars became increasingly nervous as we approached Vietnam.

Father Josef and I both expected the priest would soon demand that we turn around and go back. But it never came, and around four A.M. of our sixth day out, we came to the clearing across which was the border to Vietnam.

A good distance to the south was a Vietnamese border patrol hut. As we hid in the jungle at the edge of the clearing, Father Josef explained what we would have to do.

"The patrol is fairly lax here," he said. "But they do run spot checks, so we're going to have to be absolutely quiet."

"How about the Laotian forces?" I asked.

"There's a highway about five miles south of here that runs from Muong.Va across the border to Lai Chau in Vietnam. There's a Laotian border patrol stationed there. But they're too disorganized to run full border surveillance."

I took the field glasses from him and studied the Vietnamese border patrol post. There was a dim light shining from the hut, but at this distance I could not pick out any activity.

From where we stood in the jungle, it was at least a quarter mile across the clearing to the protection of the jungle across the border.

"We'll crawl across," Father Josef said as I lowered the glasses. "Single file. Me in the lead. And not a sound."

Father Lars and I both nodded.

Father Josef looked once again toward the border post, then nodded. "By daybreak I want to be well away from the border. So let's get on with it."

He shifted his pack to a more comfortable position, then got down on his hands and knees and crawled out to the knee-high grass in the clearing.

Father Lars went next, and I brought up the rear, the ground soft and wet.

In the darkness I could not see Father Josef, just Father Lars' backside about ten yards ahead of me.

About five minutes out, I stopped a moment to adjust the straps on my pack; they were cutting into my shoulders. When I looked up, it seemed that Father Lars had begun to swing too far to the right.

I was just about to start toward him, when a tremendous explosion lit up the night sky, the concussion lifting me off the ground and flinging me backwards.

My ears were ringing, spots danced in front of my

eyes, and blood ran down from my nose as I picked myself up.

Lights were flashing over by the Vietnamese border post, and I thought I could hear sirens.

Father Josef suddenly appeared out of the grass, his nose bleeding too, and he urgently motioned me back toward the jungle on the Laotian side.

"What about Father Lars?" I said, although I could not hear my own voice.

Father Josef shook his head. "Dead," the word formed on his lips.

We scrambled back to the jungle, and once we were within the relative safety of the trees, we got to our feet.

I could definitely hear the sirens across the clearing now, as my hearing came back.

"What the hell happened?" Father Josef snapped.

"I don't know," I said. "I stopped to fix my pack. When I looked up, it seemed like he had moved off to the right."

"Goddamn it. Goddamn it to hell," Father Josef swore. "It was a land mine. He didn't have a chance. The dirty bastards."

"I'm sorry . . ." I started, but he cut me off.

"We can't stay here. We're going to have to go north."

"We're not going back?" I asked.

"Hell no!" Father Josef snapped. "We came to rescue your POWs. We're not stopping now."

"North?"

He nodded. "China. They'll never expect us to come that way."

"Can we cross their border?"

"It'll be difficult, but I've done it before," Father Josef said. But then he looked a little closer at me. "That is if you want to continue."

I glanced back at the field. A small grass fire had started when the mine had gone off. "Let's go," I said. . . .

—From APPOINTMENT IN HAIPHONG
  A New Nick Carter Spy Thriller
  From Ace Charter In July

WHY WASTE YOUR PRECIOUS PENNIES ON GAS OR YOUR VALUABLE TIME ON LINE AT THE BOOKSTORE?

We will send you, FREE, our 28 page catalogue, filled with a wide range of Charter paperback titles—we've got something for every reader's pleasure.

Here's your chance to add to your personal library, with all the convenience of shopping by mail. There's no need to be without a book to enjoy—request your *free* catalogue today.

More Fiction Bestsellers From Ace Books!

Winners of the SPUR and WESTERN HERITAGE AWARD

Awarded annually by the Western Writers of America, the Golden Spur is the most prestigious prize a Western novel, or author, can attain.

- ☐ 22767 **FANCHER TRAIN** Amelia Bean $2.75
- ☐ 29742 **GOLD IN CALIFORNIA** Todhunter Ballard $1.75
- ☐ 47493 **LAW MAN** Lee Leighton $1.95
- ☐ 55124 **MY BROTHER JOHN** Herbert Purdum $1.95
- ☐ 72355 **RIDERS TO CIBOLA** Zollinger $2.50
- ☐ 30267 **THE GREAT HORSE RACE** Fred Grove $1.95
- ☐ 47083 **THE LAST DAYS OF WOLF GARNETT** Clifton Adams $1.95
- ☐ 82137 **THE TRAIL TO OGALLALA** Benjamin Capps $1.95
- ☐ 85904 **THE VALDEZ HORSES** Lee Hoffman $1.95

Available wherever paperbacks are sold or use this coupon.

ACE CHARTER BOOKS
P.O. Box 400, Kirkwood, N.Y. 13795

Please send me the titles checked above. I enclose $_____.
Include $1.00 per copy for postage and handling. Send check or money order only. New York State residents please add sales tax.

NAME_____

ADDRESS_____

CITY_____STATE_____ZIP_____

J. R. ROBERTS

SERIES

An all new series of adult westerns, following the wild and lusty adventures of Clint Adams, the Gunsmith!

☐ 30856	THE GUNSMITH #1: MACKLIN'S WOMEN	$2.25	
☐ 30857	THE GUNSMITH #2: THE CHINESE GUNMEN	$2.25	
☐ 30858	THE GUNSMITH #3: THE WOMAN HUNT	$2.25	
☐ 30859	THE GUNSMITH #4: THE GUNS OF ABILENE	$2.25	
☐ 30860	THE GUNSMITH #5: THREE GUNS FOR GLORY	$2.25	
☐ 30861	THE GUNSMITH #6: LEADTOWN	$2.25	

Available wherever paperbacks are sold or use this coupon.

C **ACE CHARTER BOOKS**
P.O. Box 400, Kirkwood, N.Y. 13795

Please send me the titles checked above. I enclose $ _____
Include $1.00 per copy for postage and handling. Send check or
money order only. New York State residents please add sales tax.

NAME_____

ADDRESS_____

CITY_____STATE_____ZIP_____